Special Deliverance

Other books from Scottish Cultural Press

Night Visits, Ron Butlin
1 84017 000 X

The Summer is Ended, Kenneth C Steven
1 898218 72 2

Dan, Kenneth C Steven
1 898218 07 2

Now You Must Dance, Bruce Leeming
1 898218 71 4

A World of Folk Tales from multi-cultural Scotland, Sue Stewart (ed.)
1 898218 58 7

Special Reserve: New Writing from Women in Aberdeen, Yvonne Spence (ed.)
1 898218 59 5

Special Deliverance

Donald S Murray

SCOTTISH CULTURAL PRESS
EDINBURGH

First published 1997 by
Scottish Cultural Press
Unit 14, Leith Walk Business Centre,
130 Leith Walk, Edinburgh EH6 5DT
Tel: 0131 555 5950 ◆ Fax: 0131 555 5018
e-mail: scp@sol.co.uk

British Library Cataloguing in Publication Data
A catalogue entry for this book is available from the British Library

ISBN: 1 898218 99 4

The publisher acknowledges a subsidy from the Scottish Arts Council
towards the publication of this volume

Printed and bound by
BPC-AUP Aberdeen Ltd

Contents

Acknowledgements

The short stories in this collection were – in one form or another – previously published in the following magazines: *Chapman, Radical Scotland, An Canan (West Highland Free Press Arts Supplement), Edinburgh Review, Teaching English, Northwords, Cutting Teeth, Scotland's Languages, Eilean An Fhraoich Annual*; and broadcast on BBC Radio 4 and BBC Radio Scotland.

Inspiration for the enclosed stories came from a large number of sources, but the following should be acknowledged:

'Hoover's Housekeeper' – *The Secret Life of J. Edgar Hoover* (biography).

'A Special Deliverance' – 'A Wilderness Station', Alice Munro, from the short story collection *Open Secrets* (Vintage); The Writings of James Shaw Grant (*Stornoway Gazette*), particularly on his account of 'Eathar Gabhsann' on which much of the early part of this story is based; *The French Lieutenant's Woman*, Fowles; 'The Return of Martin Guerre' (film).

'Latvians' – *The Metagama,* Jim Wilkie (Mainstream).

'The Restoration' – the work of Michael Sheehy, Crawford Gallery, Cork.

'Bird Boy' – *The Life and Death of St Kilda,* Tom Steele.

'Season and Serve' – 'The Perfect Loaf', Angus Dunn (published in the collection *Boundaries*).

Of all stories, 'Murdag' is probably the most closely based on the life of a real character. However, her story has been considerably transformed and bears no great resemblance to the actual figure.

Also to the many – especially my brother, Allan, sister, Fiona, Angus, Tom, Ian, Graham, the English Departments of both Sgoil Lionacleit, Benbecula, and the Nicolson Institute, Stornoway – whose conversation and (sometimes!) whisky helped me on my way.

Foreword

I have read many of these stories before in various magazines and I welcome this collection.

These stories are forthright and clear and some of them, for instance 'Hoover's Housekeeper', are very funny. The leap that is taken here from the CIA to gossip in Lewis is very daring and is the sort of thing that we might find in a poem. Much the same sort of thing happens in the story about Gorbachev's visit to Lewis where he sees a Lewis woman in the mould of a sturdy Russian peasant who might suit him better than the fashion-conscious and high-spending Raisa.

It may be Donald Murray's experience as a teacher that makes him write well about young people. The first story in the book, 'Bird Boy', is about a boy unhappily exiled from St Kilda. There is a story of another boy suspected by his peers of being a liar. Is he or is he not a fantasist? This is a more violent tale. It shows us among other things the global travel of the Lewis crofter-seaman.

Murray's empathy with victims is not only about people but also has to do with a dog and some stranded whales. In the story about the latter there is some casual cruelty as well.

Like many creative writers from Lewis, Murray has little time for religion. This comes out very strongly in the story which gives the book its title and which is about a minister who marries but is incapable of making love to his wife. This story is told by means of letters and fragments of pathetic English. There is violence here too as the minister hits his wife.

A reference to English is again found in a story about a woman who receives a telegram in English but is unable to read it. It is actually telling her that her son has been killed in the war. This is an interesting metaphor for imperial power and imperial language.

Thus Murray deals much with Highland themes, such as religion and language, and with a new kind of Clearance (this time from the inner cities) and set in the future.

In many of the stories there are Gaelic words and expressions.

I found them all easy to read and interesting. I am sure other readers will find the same. The detail and psychology of the tales are authentic and true to the region with which most of them deal.

Iain Crichton Smith

Son of a crofter/weaver from Ness at the north end of the Isle of Lewis, Donald S Murray spent ten years working in Glasgow as a civil servant, retail management trainee and University of Glasgow student before returning to the Western Isles – bringing his wife, Sheila, along with him from County Cork in Ireland. Since then he has not only acquired two children, Eileen and Angus, but also taught in the Nicolson Institute, Stornoway, before moving to Sgoil Lionacleit, Benbecula, where he is now Principal Teacher of English.

Dedicated to those who have been more than dedicated to me:
especially Sheila, for twenty years of love and growing;
the memory of my father, ANGUS MURRAY (1922–1981);
my children Eileen and Angus.

Bird Boy

Crouching on the edge of the school-roof, Angus stared at us with dark, resentful eyes. His face looked pinched and nervous. His thin legs with their short trousers and bruised, dirt-stained feet were like twigs stripped of bark. We gestured towards him, trying to encourage him down but his cold, grey eyes, half-hidden by the fringe of his thick brown hair, gazed as remorselessly as any sea-bird into the distance, unmoved by all our words…

The whole thing had happened so fast. One moment he was being teased by Ewan – jokes about eating seagulls and climbing cliffs – and the next he was scaling the school wall, his toes scrambling over the stonework as if each crack and bump to be found there was a step designed for him alone. He showed an agility native to all who came from St Kilda; the centuries spent on that remote Hebridean isle creating men whose heads would resolutely refuse to spin even when they peered over tall, black cliffs that crashed swiftly downwards to the sea. Nature had done its part in helping them master these heights. Like all St Kildans, Angus's ankles were wider and thicker than normal. His toes had the ability to cling and grip onto the rocks. Because of this, the school wall was only a tiny obstacle to overcome. A few seconds after leaving the ground and he was up on the slates.

And there he stayed. Macdermid, the headmaster, barked out orders, demanding he came down "this instant" while red-haired Miss Mackay, the junior teacher, twittered vainly as she tried to reason with him, her initial calmness becoming, as time went on, more than a little stirred and shaken.

There was the same reaction to our words of encouragement. "We'll be good to you," we promised. "You'll be fine." But even as we spoke, we knew our inducements were insincere – that far from wanting him to climb down from the roof, we hoped he might stay there as long as possible. On a dull January morning, it seemed far better to be out watching this strange display than inside in our classrooms scratching the headmaster's words down upon our slates. The other day, for instance, he had done little all morning except recount a long list of birds that man could eat, ranging from the usual hens, ducks and pigeons to the more exotic gannets and budgerigars. A girl had sniggered when this last species was mentioned – an act that earned her the full force of Macdermid's rage. He yanked her from her desk, tugging her thick brown hair and shouting at her till tears flooded down her face.

But today, he was a different kind of man, his face dark and troubled as he watched the newcomer to his school crouch defiantly on the roof. A bustling, bear-like figure with greasy black hair, his mouth hissed and whistled as he pondered the problem of what to do next. "I'll go and get the ladder," he finally announced, using one of the boys to help him drag it out from its place underneath the large fir tree that stood shadowing one of the windows of the school. He placed it against the wall a few inches away from Angus's feet. The boy eyed it nervously, moving a yard or so away.

It was a moment Macdermid had clearly hoped to avoid – the nervous climb up the rungs, the wobble of both wood and flesh as his portly figure made its way to the roof-edge. He stopped at the top of the ladder to speak to Angus, his words carried and enlarged by the wind.

"I know it's hard, Angus... but you've just got to get used to things. There's no possibility of returning to St Kilda. None whatsoever. That way of life is dead and buried. This is your life now... Your father working in the forestry scheme. Perhaps there is a job there for you when you leave here... You have to accept these things. They're for the best."

The headmaster's voice brought no response – a pucker of his lips, perhaps, a shudder in his breath – but apart from that, nothing. Only a tentative touch of his hand, the headmaster's attempt to gain his trust, made the boy shiver and draw back. Frightened Angus might fall, Macdermid drew his fingers quickly away.

"You're sure you won't come down?" he pleaded.

There was no reply. A few moments later and Macdermid's huge bulky form stomped down the ladder. Back on earth among us, he shook his head at his failure to bring the boy with him. It was not a reaction that lasted too long, however, for a short time afterwards his usual brusque manner was restored. He shouted his orders at us, knowing we would all scurry and obey.

"Ewan! Seeing you're partly responsible for this, you try and bring him down. Go up the ladder and talk to him. Douglas! Go and ask the carrier if we can borrow some transport. Someone needs to go to the estate and bring back Angus's father. He might be able to bring his son down."

While the rest of us were dashing about obeying Macdermid's commands, Miss Mackay was speaking to one of the two old spinsters whose house stood next to the school. Her words were low and intimate, the hushed, whispering sound of a secret being shared.

"They should never have come here," she said. "What did those people know of a place like this? Trees, an open road, the mountains... When all they were used to was the sea, the cliffs, birds flying over their heads... And, of course, to cap it all, the government sends them to work on a forestry scheme. They could have shown more sense. These folk had never even seen a tree before they arrived here."

In the meantime, Ewan was standing at the top of his ladder, apologising for all his wrongs. A fat, red-haired, freckle-faced boy, he was much more used to being a victim than a bully. His legs shook as he stood high above us.

"I'm sorry..." he sobbed, "I didn't mean to hurt your feelings... I promise I didn't... I won't..."

Halfway through his explanations, Angus's head turned away. His eyes had become fixed on a hooded crow which had landed – its wings swishing – on the far end of the roof. Boy and bird studied one another with great interest, their bodies stilled by mutual curiosity. Slowly, Angus turned round, rising on his haunches as though he were planning to trap the bird the instant it took flight. He inched his way forward noiselessly, both his hands outstretched.

Before he had time to move very far, the crow took off, shaking its feathers for an instant before it rushed into the air, landing on the top branch of the tree that stood beside the school. It was only there for a moment before it flew away again, but throughout the whole of that time, Angus's gaze never left the creature. He took his time studying it – the sheen of its wings, the steadfastness of its gaze – as if it were a fulmar he was sizing for a catch. As it flew away, high above the forestry scheme and towards the blue, heather-topped hills of Morvern, his eyes continued to follow the movement of its flight.

It was from this direction that Angus's father came a short time later, his hands still soiled from his labours. A tall, slight man with thick, brown hair and wind-flushed features, he was so thin the veins and sinews in his neck stood out as he craned his head to listen to Macdermid. Words passed between the two men; explanations made and accepted. As the St Kildan's English was halting and slow, each brief silence was hastily filled by the headmaster.

"We have tried our best to bring him down, but sadly it has proved beyond us. He has reacted suspiciously towards our every gesture, rejecting even the offers of friendship the children have made." Macdermid paused briefly, drawing himself to his full height. "We were wondering if you could do something to help bring all this to an end. The whole situation has disturbed the work of the school for long enough."

"Yes... yes... I'm sorry, headmaster, for all the bother we've been causing... Sorry, sorry..."

But for all the clumsiness of his English, there was an eagerness to his step. He climbed the ladder nimbly – secure and confident on each rung. When he reached the top, he stood for a moment silently. Shaking his head sadly, he then began to speak.

"Aonghais."

The Gaelic word for Angus was said gently – as if it were a plea or a note of despair. The boy looked up, biting his bottom lip to keep it from trembling.

"Thig a nuas," his father said.

"Come down." The St Kildan's words were translated by Miss Mackay who mouthed them, almost unwittingly, as she stood on the playground below. Angus did not move, however. Instead, he shook his head, his face as impassive as ever.

"Aonghais," he said again – this time with greater urgency.

The boy's eyes jerked upwards, looking at his father's face. He began to speak rapidly – a flurry of explanations rushing from his mouth. It was impossible to make out what he was saying, yet easy to hazard a guess. He was talking once again of the cliffs of his native island, the fulmars and gannets that veered and screeched around them, rising on the tide of air that swirled and eddied above the waters pounding upon the rocks.

And his father's reply to all this? That was an attempt to reason with this vision, no doubt informing his son that these times would never return, but even as he spoke, trying desperately to persuade him of this, his words were undermined by the lack of conviction in his own voice. He, too, longed for these cliffs. That feeling was present in all his denials, weakening all the reassurance he was trying his best to give.

"Cha till na laithean sin tuilleadh," he declared, informing him those days would never return. And then he reached out his hand to bring his son down. "Trobhad... Come on."

Yet while he waited for his answer, something happened. A movement distracted Angus, his gaze switching in the direction of the tree. A pigeon had settled there, hidden in the shadow of the branches like a sea-bird nesting in the blackness of a cliff. The young boy's body grew taut as he watched it, becoming tense and alert. Rising to his haunches, he said one word to his father. It was the Gaelic for "bird".

"Eun."

4

"Dè...?" his father mumbled, wondering what he was on about.

Angus pressed a finger against his mouth, trying to silence the older man. "Eun," he repeated, and then in English, a memory from Macdermid's lesson a few days before: "Pigeons we can eat."

And before his father could reach out a hand to restrain him, the boy was away. His feet padded softly as he crept towards the place where the bird sat preening the puffed-out feathers of its chest. On one occasion, a small stone shifted from where it had been lodged by the vibration of Angus's footsteps a short distance below, but this only halted him for an instant. Knowing the bird had not been disturbed, he continued to move forward.

He only paused when he came to the length of ledge immediately alongside the tree. His eyes narrowed, measuring the gap between its nearest branches and the roof. Slowly he drew himself to almost his full height, his body poised and ready for the jump. One or two steps...

And then there was the leap...

He flew towards the tree, jumping the yard or two between its branches and the school wall as he must have leapt over wider distances on St Kilda, the sea hundreds of yards below his feet, but this time there was no rock he could cling onto at the end of his flight – only the branches of a tree that dipped and dived with the impact of his weight, veering down towards the earth and then jerking him speedily upwards. In his terror, he barely noticed the pigeon flying away, its wings fast and fearful. Instead, he only heard the crack of wood, the breaking branch, the rush of air as he crashed to the ground, striking the playground gravel with a horrifying smack. A few moments later, the brown grit of its surface began to darken and turn red...

He never climbed after that...

When the others reached his side that day, they found a bone protruding from a gash in his knee cap. The wound never healed properly. For years afterwards, he limped around the hills of Morvern helping those who worked on the forestry scheme with the occasional piece of light work, the odds and ends that needed doing. As he walked, his body dipped to the left. "Like a boat listing," Ewan would say, describing him in later life. "The man's weighed down with eating sea-birds. Too much cargo to the side." And he would jab his listener's ribs with a fleshy elbow as he said this, never having lost his weakling's talent for poking fun at those less lucky than himself.

But if Angus ever overheard him, he would never let on. He would continue working till the arrival of dusk or a surge of pain prevented him. On occasions like these, he would use a stick to get around, placing his whole weight on a piece of wood as frail as the one which had failed him all these years before.

It was a harsh life for someone who had once been agile and athletic, but there was a strange sort of comfort in it too. It was his father who used to point this out, puffing his pipe as he sat among the other men at the forestry scheme talking and swapping tales. "He's never talked about going back to St Kilda since he falled," he would say. "He's free of thinking about the island."

And from the way the old man's eyes would moisten with tears, it was easy to see that this was a freedom he would never achieve. He would go to his grave longing for days he knew only too well could never return.

Hoover's Housekeeper

"A deep gloom settled over the village of Cairnbost recently when it was discovered that its most celebrated citizen, Miss Nora Jemima Macaulay, had passed away at her home in Orange County, California..."

With these words, the *Maransay Chronicle* announced the death of Nora Jemima – a "celebrated citizen" whom no-one in the village could remember. There was good reason for this. Ever since the early twenties when she headed west on the émigré ship, the *Sedna,* she had never returned home. Yet despite her long absence, Nora never suffered the symptoms of amnesia that often affected those exiled even a handful of years. From her various homes throughout the States, she kept herself informed of all that was happening in her native village – her knowledge gained by virtue of the fact that, as the *Maransay Chronicle* reported in her obituary:

> *For many years, Nora worked as cook and housekeeper in the home of the former director of the United States' Federal Bureau of Investigation, the late J. Edgar Hoover.*

It was not, however, her inquiring mind that gained her this employment. It was, instead, her skills in the kitchen that first drew her to the attention of the young law enforcement officer. In his early years as director, he had taken on a long succession of cooks – each of whom had disappointed him in some way. A plateful of ravioli would, for instance, find him wrinkling his pug-nose in the suspicion that a member of his staff was an agent for the Mafia. A serving of Beef Stroganoff would inform him that his cook was possibly in the pay of the Soviets. Even a helping of Irish stew could be put aside and treated as suspect; maybe this one was in the service of that troublesome Boston Catholic family, the Kennedys.

Into the turmoil of his kitchen came Nora. From the beginning of her time there, the young Hebridean won the trust of her boss. Her servings of herring and potatoes could be chewed over with ease; her porridge swallowed without the thought that it might, somehow, be ideologically suspect. Even in his most paranoid moments, the idea that anyone with dangerous, foreign ideas – like Socialism or Communism – could ever manage to produce a simple joint of mutton never passed through Hoover's head. Instead, he relished her Scotch broth, scones and oatcakes; a smile coming to his thick, heavily-jowled face as every evening he anticipated the arrival of her meals.

"My... my... my..." he would say as he tucked into yet another of her dinners. "You're a wonderful cook. A lady with amazing culinary skills."

She would shy at his compliments, shrinking into the slight, mouse-like girl she always appeared to be in his company. "My mother taught me well," she'd reply.

"She sure did. She sure did," J. Edgar would grin as he rose from the table, setting off to plan yet another arrest in defence of the nation's security. "And I am truly grateful for it."

It was only a matter of time, however, before Nora's other talents were recognised. That moment came one evening when Hoover stepped into the kitchen to prepare a cheese sandwich for himself. Lying beside the bread-bin was a letter Nora was writing to her sister, Marsalli Anne. J. Edgar lifted it in his fingers, reading it with an increasing sense of interest:

"...Is Willie Maclean still drinking? How is his wife putting up with it? Is she still unhappy, still telling her stories to Ishbal Mairi down the road? How on earth does she trust that one? Doesn't she know she's spreading stories all over the place...?"

The more Hoover read, the more he recognised a mind just like his own; the only difference between them was of scale. He smiled at this, marvelling at the thought that an intelligence so perfectly complementing his could be found within the walls of his home.

It was while he stood there reading her letter that she walked in. He noticed her right away, his dark eyes fixing her with the same intense expression that had intimidated so many in the past.

"You're some lady, aren't you?" he grinned.

She said nothing to this, unsure whether to take his words as a compliment or a prelude to being fired.

"I think we can use you," he said. "There's this job where I need someone I can trust..."

Apparently, there was a local politician in Pittsburgh who was deeply involved in a number of graft and corruption cases. He needed someone placed within his household to gather evidence against the man.

"A cook..." he smiled, the broad outline of his body framed in the kitchen doorway. "A cook's the ideal person. After all, the way to any man's trust is through his taste buds."

She laughed at this, agreeing to do as he wanted. In a matter of months, the task was complete; the politician on his way to prison as a result of a conversation she had overheard at his dinner table. Hoover was delighted at her success, the dark, almost Negroid face – which he had spent many hours in his youth attempting to scrub white – beaming as he welcomed her back to his home.

"What can I do for you?" he declared. "How can I reward you for all the help you have given?"

In an instant, Nora knew her answer. For some time, she had been troubled over the reliability of her reports from Cairnbost. She knew too well that Marsalli Anne could hardly be described as an independent witness. She could be concealing information about her own problems; the fact that her husband, John Murchadh Martin, drank overmuch; that her children – Lachlann, Nora and Finlay – were plaguing her with troubles. It was the thought of these little gaps in her knowledge that made her make a strange request of Hoover. Would he send a few of his G-men over to Scotland to keep an eye on her fellow-villagers...? The FBI director smiled in response.

"Is that all you want?"

Nora Jemima nodded.

"Of course, lady. We can easily do that for you."

It was as a result of this agreement that, from the early 1930s onward, strange visitors began to appear in and around the village of Cairnbost. They would turn up on days when the local people were taking home peats for their winter fires, or their fank was full of sheep for the clipping. Somewhere in their possession would be a notepad, set of binoculars, a camera or two. The villagers would watch in wonder as their every word and movement was observed and noted.

"Towerists!" they would declare contemptuously.

"...or Hollywood looking for fresh talent!" the young girls would fantasise, putting on their best dresses for a day out on the moor.

But in the files they sent back to Washington, there was much to disturb Nora. Tales of tiny, red-haired John Murchadh Martin and his drunken exploits. How he had deliberately lowered his trousers in front of the American observers and their cameras. (The photographic evidence was enclosed in the file.) How he had declared his support for Communism in a drink-fired argument. How he had composed a love-song in honour of Stalin and Lenin, singing it in the bar of the local hotel. And, worst of all, there was the time he yelled at an inquisitive neighbour: "You're worse than that creep who's my sister's boss. J. Edgar bloody Hoover!"

Nora read these words in a mixture of terror and dismay. Having a brother-in-law like John Murchadh Martin could easily undermine her position in the Hoover household. Yet there were worse consequences than that. She could imagine mocking voices in the backrooms of the Senate and the White House. "How can we trust a man who offers employment in his own home to those whose relatives are fellow-travellers of the Reds?" She didn't know how Hoover could manage to answer that question. After all, it was similar to those which he and his fellow G-men had probably asked in a thousand interrogations, using the same words again and again while their suspects sweated under a harsh and glaring light.

The thought of all this troubled Nora for weeks. She made mistakes in her cooking: forgetting to salt the potatoes; letting a pan of milk boil over. There was even one time she broke one of her own cardinal rules and accepted another woman's advice in cooking, adding a dash of paprika to a pot-full of stew. Hoover's fork paused halfway to his mouth that evening, his eyes following her for a long time before he finally glanced away. It was as if he were starting to suspect her of falling for the harsh ideologies that had overcome much of Europe; the red flare of their flags and emblems tainting even his enjoyment of his evening meal.

It was then she decided to approach him – to tell him of the brother-in-law whose senses had long been subverted by the combined effects of Karl Marx and whisky. She twisted her fingers as she told her story, letting him know that her main concern was the effect it might have on Hoover's own position. The FBI director, however, only smiled grimly when she had finished her tale.

"I'll have a word with Clyde about it," he said, referring to Mr Tolson, his closest colleague in the Bureau. Nora had even seen the two of them dressed in female clothes in her employer's bedroom one morning some months before. "We're off to a fancy dress party," Hoover had explained, and she had thought no more about it – apart from the fact it was an odd way of behaving at that time of day.

She stood around, waiting for him to say more, but he never did. Instead, his gaze shifted back to the pile of papers on his desk, the blankness of his expression informing her the interview was over. She went to bed that night still fearful and uncertain, hoping that behind her employer's impassive face, a solution was being considered.

And then, within a month or so, there came an end to her troubles.

She read about her brother-in-law's death in a letter from Marsalli Anne. Apparently, a tragic accident had occurred one afternoon when John Murchadh had gone out to gather a few stray sheep from an area of common grazing near the shore. Around four hours later, a search-party left the village to discover where he, too, might have strayed, finding him washed up on some rocks with a half-bottle in his back pocket. "How many times did I warn him about drinking?" Marsalli asked mournfully in her letter, "but he never ever listened to me."

From that day, Nora Jemima was never quite so certain about the world in which she lived. Unsure of the answers she might find to her questions, she chose not to ask any, serving, instead, plates of roast beef he would savour; desserts he might relish; cups of coffee he was able to sip and enjoy. And, of course, in the spare time she had left, she continued to chronicle the life of Cairnbost – her obsession with its activities sending out Federal Agents who would try and blend with the locals chatting at the counter of the village shop, recording their quarrels and disagreements on tape recorders disguised within briefcases, or continuing to post long epistles filled with questions to the home of Marsalli Anne.

As the years went on, the contents of these changed a great deal. Old names disappeared, and new ones – the children of her own generation – took their place. Yet despite this, Nora mailed her letters with the same fervour as before, filing each reply away in huge, dust-covered folios in the housekeeper's quarters in Hoover's home. And when she came to leave there, after Hoover died in the spring of 1972, these went with her, shifting with all her other possessions to her own house in Orange County. She spent her final days there as the last surviving member of her family – a fact that the *Maransay Chronicle* noted in her obituary, adding that:

> *Nevertheless, she still kept in contact with her nieces and nephews on the island. The sympathy of the community is with them at this time, particularly her sister Marsalli's son, Lachlann, who, together with his wife, Lorna, was out visiting his aunt in California at the time of her demise.*

Yet there was more to the end of her life-story than the local correspondent of the *Maransay Chronicle* could ever have imagined. Her death occurred only a week after Lachlann and Lorna arrived on their Hoover free-flight to California (obtained after they had bought a washing machine for their home). They had been met by a small, white-haired lady whose vitality belied the fact she was in her late eighties. Her voice drilled questions incessantly into their ears:

"How's Mairi Maggie? Is she still carrying on with that fellow down the road? Is it true he left his wife behind in Glasgow? Did they have any children? Do they ever…?"

But the splendour of her home soon made up for the discomfort of their arrival. Lachlann stood in awe at the sight of the tiger-skin rug in the hallway; his mouth sagged as he stood before her jacuzzi; his eyes could only roll in wonder when he saw a dozen or so sprinklers form a multitude of rainbows on her lawn.

"It's amazing!" he kept saying. "No wonder you never came home."

But later on, there was the night when, looking for a toilet, he stepped into her study by mistake. Switching on the light, he saw the huge folios stacked upon its shelves. "Cairnbost 1929"; "Cairnbost 1930"; "Cairnbost 1931"; the titles on their bindings read. He picked one up – the chronicle for 1934, the year his father died – and turned its pages over.

What happened after that can only be supposition. Did he flick through the papers to discover the photo of John Murchadh with his Long Johns at his ankles? Did he scan the FBI agents' reports of his father's actions – the many drunken exploits and remarks noted in the book? Did he discover, too, his mother's letter, informing Nora of her husband's death? And did he, standing there as dawn broke over the western coastline of North America, twist the accounts of these events over and over in his mind till they formed certain hard and definite conclusions? And was his reaction then to turn upon his aunt in a bitter, vengeful rage…?

There are only a few things known for certain about all this.

The following morning, Nora Jemima was found dead at the foot of the stairway in her home. A fortnight later, her obituary appeared in the *Maransay Chronicle.*

Canna

It was only after my father's funeral that I headed out to release Canna from her confinement. I wasn't even near the door when her barking and whining began; displaying an odd mixture of grief and excitement as she scrambled in the barn. As I put the key in the lock, she was up on her back legs, scratching at the wood.

"Lie down, Canna," I said as I allowed the daylight in… and the dog out. Canna darted between my legs as if I weren't there – our old black and white collie rushing towards the door of our home. I could only curse my own carelessness as I followed in her trail; I should have expected that to happen. For the three nights the wake had been held in our house, she had wailed for hours on end, even disturbing our neighbours at two and three in the morning with her cries. It should have been obvious that after she had been allowed out, she would dash for our door, desperate to see her master once again.

By the time I arrived in the kitchen, she had created a few problems I had to solve. My mother was standing in the kitchen, barely in control of her temper. When she shouted for the dog, her voice was dry and broken.

"Canna! Canna! Come back!"

It took only a glance to make out what had happened. The dog had entered one of her "forbidden zones" – the inside of our sitting room. When I went in there, the dog was circling the room, sniffing each corner of her surroundings. Time after time she would stop briefly where my father always sat, thrusting her head into his empty chair.

"How often have I told that animal not to go in there?" Mum said. "But she's looking for your Dad. She won't listen to me. She won't ever listen to me…"

After things had calmed down, I took Canna for a walk, heading down the croft to the shore. As we passed the crops my father had planted, she rushed and tumbled, racing in zigzags down the middle of our land.

"Good dog," I muttered, flattered by the affection she was displaying towards me. Yet at the same time, I kept thinking how much the dog was going to miss my father. They spent so much time together; Canna at his side as he worked on the sheep. In a hundred different tasks – from the docking

13

of tails to the butchering of the animals – the dog wasn't far away. She would obey his every word and gesture, never even questioning his occasional show of bad temper when, somehow or other, the flock broke loose of their control. He would shout and yell then, blaming the dog for his own worst mistakes.

But Canna might have sensed what I had always known – the kindness that was in him, even when his moods were at their darkest and most uneven. One of my aunts had tried to explain what caused the distant look that slipped over his eyes at these times. "He's had his troubles, you know. Your mother's been a hard woman to live with – ever since you were born…" Yet when I questioned her about this, she refused to explain. "That stupid mouth of mine. I've always opened it far too wide."

I sat down on the grass, thinking of the strange and silent home in which I had been raised. When I was younger, I had once or twice caught my parents in an argument. "You're being pig-headed as usual," I remember my Dad saying, his hands becoming fists and his knuckles white and cold as he leaned forward in his sitting-room chair. It was then that Mum spotted me, standing in the half-open doorway in my pyjamas. She pointed a finger in my direction, and – if my memory doesn't fool me – a smile came to her face.

"The wee fellow's here," she said.

My father shook his head angrily and left his seat. A few moments later, the back door slammed. He was heading out to the barn where he spent most of his time.

The memory faded as Canna began to lick my fingers. I smiled and tousled the animal's head. She cocked her ears and whined softly, looking up at me with sad, brown eyes. It was that expression that made me start to fool myself – thinking I could replace my father as the centre of the dog's life. She would follow my footsteps as faithfully as she had once haunted his…

My self-deception did not last long.

So many things had been forgotten in the yearnings of that moment – my job in the council, working for Environmental Health; the stirrings of my first, truly serious romance; even the fact I hated the relentless monotony of croft-work. Within weeks of my father's death, poor Canna was reduced to spending most of her time lying on the kitchen or the barn-floor, my resolution long forgotten. For a while, my mother said nothing, apparently unaware of the fact that I was neglecting the croft and animals we owned. But one evening, it became clear little had escaped her notice. Sitting

14

opposite me at the kitchen table, she decided it was time to speak.

"We'll have to get rid of the sheep."

"What?" I muttered.

"We'll have to get rid of most of the sheep," she said again. "There's no one here to look after them any more. You've got your job. I'm not fit to do much with them. We'll have to let most of them go, only keeping a few for the freezer. That's about all we can manage."

To begin with, I protested, spluttering about how Dad wouldn't like it. He had put his heart and soul into the sheep... But she kept on arguing, giving me that look I had so often seen defeat my father. And then, there were the arguments she put forward – each one more logical than the last. I couldn't deny there was no-one around to watch over the sheep; to keep an eye on them when they were ill or lambing. I couldn't even deny the fact that I hadn't exactly spent much time on them during the previous few weeks. I shrugged my shoulders wearily as I gave in to her words.

For all that, it wasn't easy to let the sheep go. We advertised in the local paper and a crofter from one of the neighbouring villages arrived at our door. Seeking profit from our family's loss, he haggled for a long time over the price and the animals he would take. Eventually, though, we came to an agreement. A sum was set and paid for the main part of the flock.

I went out with Canna to gather them. The dog raced in circles as I shouted out my signals, rushing to the left when I wanted her right; going right when I indicated the opposite. There were times, too, when she acted in ways she had never done with my father – nipping in front of the sheep and lunging at their heads. This would stop them going forward, forcing them to run back in my direction. And all the time, the purchaser of the animals looked on, grinning at my antics.

"I can see why you want to get rid of them," he said. "That dog's worse than useless."

Eventually, however, we managed to gather the flock together, putting them in a makeshift pen and lifting them out, one after the other, into the trailer of his tractor. We filled this twice, watching for a long time as he journeyed down the road to his home.

It was only then I allowed myself to wonder what Dad would have thought of this – all his time and slow efforts coming to an end with the speed of money changing hands. Late that night, I heard, for the first time in months, Canna's crying echoing from the barn. It was almost as if she knew what was happening – that the letting-go of the sheep was condemning her to a new uselessness, a waste of her instincts and skills. As I went to sleep, the animal was still howling. It seemed that nothing could comfort her now.

Canna was to cause me further problems. When I arrived home a few weeks later, the grazings clerk was there to greet me. It was his duty to see to the running of the common grazings, adjudicate on quarrels such as the division of peat-banks or the dividing line between two crofts. It didn't take long to discover what had brought him to my door.

"That dog of yours has been worrying sheep," he said. "When you're out at work, she's out on the moor, chasing the animals this way and that. You've got to keep control of her. Otherwise, the next time she's seen out there, it's the bullet for her. There's no doubt about that."

What could I say but "sorry"? As I guided him to the door, I mumbled my apologies, promising I would keep her tied while away at work. The grazings clerk nodded gravely at this, averting his gaze from Canna as he made his way from our home.

There was no sign of such unease in my mother as she waited for me to come back in. A week or two before, she had complained about the dog-hair on the kitchen floor when the dog had been moulting. Now, she saw the chance of getting rid of its source.

"Well?" she said shortly.

She sat down opposite me, her hands crossed on the kitchen table as she waited for my reply.

"I've been told to keep Canna under control," I answered.

She stretched out her hands, flexing her fingers. "And is that possible?"

"Of course. We can keep her tied all day."

"And what then? Tell me. Are we ever going to use the animal again?" She shook her head. "I mean, she was of some use before – when your Dad was alive – I'll give you that. But now? We've hardly got any sheep. Even when you're out with the animal, you can't control her. Tell me honestly. What's the point of keeping her? If you're only doing it out of sentiment, you'd be best to get rid of the beast."

It was useless to argue. Even I could see the cold, hard logic of her words. Impossible, too, to quarrel with that stare that seemed to lay bare all your weakness, exposing all that you valued as soft, sentimental and worthless. I reacted to her argument in much the same way as my father had done all those years before. My knuckles white and cold, hands becoming fists, I rose from my seat.

"So you want me to do it? Get rid of her? Is that what you want me to do?"

She withdrew her hands from the table, using them to prop her chin. "There's no alternative," she said.

I shook my head in exasperation. A few moments later, the door slammed behind me.

"Canna!"

As soon as her name left my lips, the dog was at my heel. She looked rounder than she had done a few months before; her coat seemed to have lost most of its usual sheen. Yet she sprinted along beside me as I walked down the croft; bolting through holes in the fence where the mesh gaped wide, her body tense and low when there were sheep nearby.

Her movements reminded me of my father. I could picture Canna and him working together, gathering the sheep. A small, brown-haired man whose stocky frame already gave some sign of the heart condition that would one day kill him, he would yell and wave his arms as some ewe with her lamb at foot spilled out from the flock.

"Canna!" he would shout. "Faigh i!"

In a flurry of activity, the dog would obey, herding them back with the others. We would hear them bleating as the flock moved on – Canna keeping them running only a short distance away until they reached the village boundary. Then she would deliberately rush them, dispersing the sheep this way and that out on the moor.

It was while doing work like this my father had been content, away from a marriage that had long been cold and comfortless. Instead, he had turned his attentions towards his croft – the hours spent there being a kind of infidelity, one that brought him its own comforts and rewards. As each year passed, there would be a fresh lot of lambs. There would be, too, a field full of oats, green and tall as they swept round my young body; crops of potatoes and turnips would also stand tall and splendid at my side.

And now there was this – a lonely walk through a barren, empty landscape. There was only one possible end to it – the place my fellow-villagers called Geo na Coin. It lay at the foot of a deep crack among the dark cliffs that formed much of the village coastline. On the boulders at its base, a few cormorants stood, studying the waves for fish they might eat. No doubt there were times when they obtained richer, more unusual fare – the flesh of animals that crofters had tossed down – for this was the place where people had traditionally thrown their unwanted dogs and cats to their deaths.

It was my turn to go there – to tie a rope and stone around my dog Canna's neck. I knew that as I did this, my fingers would tremble and shake; my father's form appear in my mind, working the croft with the dog at his side; that I would feel, too, a sense of betrayal, putting an end to the last tangible form of his love for the land. But I knew, too, that I would have to do it. The realities of my life; my mother's insistent voice: all these things gave me little choice.

Latvians

Gaelic was my language of innocence. Of psalms, songs and faith. The minister in his pulpit, his round collar barely seen under the heavy jowls of his chin. "Is e Dia fèin a's buachaill dhomh…" we would sing. "Cha bhi mi ann an dìth…" Or my father kneeling before his fireside chair, his right hand thumbing the spine of a large, black Bible. "A Dhia… Dhia… Thoir cuideachadh dhuinn…" he would mutter. Each phrase was a desperate plea for help, his whole body trembling with what he sensed was his unworthiness for such assistance.

Yet I have long since turned my back on that tongue. English has been the language of my experience. I heard it first in the schoolroom – alien and strange – and it still echoes in the streets of the city where I now live – "O Canada…" – with its babble of tongues, its medley of voices. Nowadays its vowels and consonants rest easily on my tongue, yet occasionally, when I hear a rush of unintelligible sounds coming from the mouth of some newly-arrived Chinese or Indian immigrant, I can still remember how it felt to be unfamiliar with the language in which I write these words.

It was on the boat that took me to these shores that I first tried to master its intricacies. On the emigrant ship, *Sedna*, I spent most of my time away from those who, like me, had left the islands. Instead, I sought the company of those who came from other places – the crewmen who hailed from England, Ireland or the Scottish mainland; the passengers from distant countries who had boarded the ship before the onslaught of Hebrideans joined them at Maransay pier. It was a way of practising the language in which I still felt so uneasy, of coming to terms with its difficulties before I arrived on land.

Among the foreigners was a young and attractive woman. The first I saw of her was when she arrived on deck with her parents a day after we had left Maransay; one moment she was in the shadow of the doorway and the next, the slim lines of her body could be seen in silhouette against the blueness of the sky. The paleness of her face was framed in the gold lace of her hair as she turned round to ask an old, stout woman in a thick, black coat to hurry down some steps. I felt a shock pass through me as I watched her – the impact of her beauty like a sharp gust blowing across the ocean. Most of all, there was the surprise of seeing the whiteness of her hands. Their paleness and grace was extraordinary. Most of the women I had known before had fingers which were either red or chapped or misshapen. Compared to theirs, hers were long and flawless.

After that first day, I used to watch her continually, comforting myself with the minor imperfections she revealed. One of her top teeth was ever so slightly crooked. There was a sorrowful quality about her expression, her lips continually set in a frown. There were times, too, when her voice seemed more than a little strident and a stream of incomprehensible words left her lips in a high-pitched whine... These tiny flaws made her less inaccessible than before. As each of these details were noted, I hoped that the time would come when I would be able to cast aside my shyness, and begin to talk to her. In the meantime, I continued to cling to the stretch of deck-rail where I stood every day, watching both her and the woman whom I imagined, from a distance, to be her mother. It was a stance which my fellow-islanders mocked, nudging my ribs with sharpened elbows.

"What on earth are you doing hanging about near her?" they would jeer. "She isn't going to give a clown like you a second glance."

"Oh, you never know... You never know." I would wink, mimicking a confidence I did not possess.

The other lads laughed at this, ridiculing even the idea that a foreign lady could take an interest in one of their own. They would grin on every occasion they saw me in their vicinity. "Cum ort leis," they would laugh, urging me on in my efforts. After this, they would return to one of the lower parts of the deck where the emigrants from the islands had all gathered, singing sentimental songs of the land they had just left. It was a nostalgia I did not share. "Home" meant some good things to me – that much was true – but most of all, it meant poverty, the savage cruelty of its land and ocean. It meant the thin, barren soil which men like my brother had raided after the Great War from the acres of farmland that had once existed on the site of our village... and which despite all his labours, had rewarded him with a bare and meagre harvest. I was glad to be leaving. There was little there to keep me.

But the New World... that had much of the same fascination as the girl. There was the appeal of the mysterious, the attraction of the distant and most of all, as in these hands I had glimpsed, what I imagined to be a flawless perfection. I needed to get close to examine its faults and failings, the blemishes on the skin. After this, it might be possible to judge matters more accurately – to come to some conclusions of my own...

20

It was a storm that allowed me to do this with the girl. One evening the wind began to rise and sent the waves sprawling. Every moment seemed to bring another roll of the boat, a further deluge lashing against the deck. It was while I stood there sheltering against an outside cabin wall that I noticed the girl rushing across the deck. An instant later and her foot slipped... She tumbled into one of the many pools that had gathered on the steel surface of the deck.

There was no rush to lift her up. The swaying of the boat and the dampness of the deck made any sudden movement like this impossible. Instead I moved slowly and carefully. When I reached out to take her arm, I felt her body stiffen and rebel. It was clear she didn't want anyone to lift her. Still, I persisted, talking softly to her in a language she clearly did not understand.

"Fuirich... Togaidh mi thu."

After a moment, she allowed me to do just as I had said, raising her to her feet. I felt the dampness of her coat as I did so, its fine fabric soaked by her fall. Even her hair was wet; some of its strands sticking firmly to her cheek.

"Are you all right?" I asked.

"Yes," she nodded, a frown hard on her face. "I am fine."

With that, she walked away from me, looking – as even I could see – slightly ridiculous as she swayed from side to side of the deck with a large damp stain covering most of the length of her coat. As she walked away, trying her best to hold herself rigid and proud, an English crewman I had met came up to me and slapped his hand on my shoulder.

"Isn't she a beauty now?" he grinned. "I do believe our proud Russian has just fallen for you." He chortled happily at his own joke as he, too, walked away, going about his duties with a broad smile on his face.

It was the word "Russian" that troubled me about this conversation. Our minister had mentioned them in his sermons. "Chan eil iad a' creidsinn ann an Dia," he had shouted, claiming they were atheists. "Mharbh iad an righ aca," he had thundered, blaming every one of them for the assassination of the Tsar. Fearing that she was one of this godless, murdering group, I kept away from her for days. It was impossible to know how she might react to the help I had given her. She could see me as a possible convert to the Bolshevik cause or else as a likely enemy. Either position seemed dangerous to occupy.

There was more than this, however, that made me keep my distance. There was the way in which she reacted to my offer of help – like an angry dog tensing at the touch of my fingers. Another move and she could turn on me, snapping with rage. For all my innocence – and her obvious beauty – I decided she was a woman to be avoided. There was that air of righteousness about her, a coldness that defied everyone's approach.

I could see this even with the woman whom I thought was her mother. The old woman crept slowly behind her and not once did the "Russian" girl falter in her steps to offer her any assistance. A child crying on deck did not draw one sympathetic glance. She barely noticed his existence, moving on as swiftly as she could.

Yet a few days later, she was the one who approached me, stopping me as I walked around the deck.

"I… would… like… to… thank… you," she smiled.

She talked as though she had just learned this speech from a phrase book; each word halting and slow. I nodded nervously in response. Despite myself, I felt very pleased by this unexpected show of gratitude.

"It was nothing," I said.

She smiled again, a little stiffly, and then turned to go. It was on impulse that I reached out to restrain her, touching her arm as I had when I lifted her to her feet. There was the same reaction as before; her body becoming rigid and stiff.

"I didn't know you were a Russian," I said.

There was little that could have prepared me for the way in which she greeted my words. Her pale features darkened at once, replaced by a flush of red. "I am not a Russian," she said, her teeth clenched tightly. "I am a Latvian."

"I'm sorry…" I began. "I didn't know…"

"Sorry." She repeated my apology. "That's the matter. Nobody knows the difference between being Russian and being Latvian. Nobody knows. And yet there is big difference. Big difference."

Her finger was waving as she was talking – the hand that had once seemed fine and flawless now wagged in my direction, reinforcing the lecture she was giving. I stood silently before her, aware that her whole performance was capturing the attention of a ship's officer standing nearby. Doubtless, he was wondering what was going on.

"We are a small country," she continued, "trying to live in peace. Yet near us there are many big – what word would you use…?" She paused as she tried to think of it. "Bullies. Big countries like Poland, Germany, Russia. They would make my father's estates a battlefield for their big armies."

I nodded, even though I sensed that any reaction of mine was completely unnecessary. She was in the pulpit. It was my task simply to listen to the sermon she was giving. And I did this well enough, even though every event and place of which she spoke seemed far remote from the island which up until then had been my home. There were no surrounding armies to threaten its borders – only the recruiting officer who seemed to come for each passing generation, offering their promises to any young man who might be coaxed into an uniform. My own brother, Eoin, had been among the ones taken in by this. When he signed up for the Great War, he had been offered land for his part in the fight.

"It is only since the last war... since the Kaiser and the Tsar fell... that we have at last gained our freedom." She continued to speak, her voice now as shrill as a whisper. "And do you know what we have done with it?

"We have turned upon ourselves," she said vigorously, her eyes brimming with tears. "The peasants... the peasants who have so long worked upon my father's estates... They break down the walls that surround my father's farm and they take his land for themselves. They build their houses there!"

It was these words that startled me into recognition – that made a distant nation suddenly similar to my own. They made me think of my brother – of how he had been without land for years, waiting for the government to fulfil the promises they had made before the beginning of the war until, finally, one day, his patience had come to an end. Together with a number of others, he had broken through the walls of a neighbouring farm. He had claimed his own stretch of ground there, building his new home with the stones of the boundary he had just broken through.

"These people! They take the land that has been in my family for generations. They take every centimetre that my father has watched over and cared for all his life. And do you know what will happen? Do you know what will happen now they have this land?"

"No." I blurted out my answer, still thinking of my brother and how he had gained this land for himself and his family.

"They will ruin it!" she said, her voice hissing. "Within a few years, no crops will grow. Even the pasture will have turned to weeds. And do you know why? Do you know why?" There was a quick burst of breath before she gave me her answer. "Because these people are lazy! They do not know how to work!"

"No!" The image of my brother was in my mind as I shouted. He was standing in a field of oats, a scythe in his hands. Sweat was trickling down his face; large, damp stains soaking his shirt, yet he was still determined to continue, ignoring the way we would often urge him to rest. "These people are not lazy! They know how to work!" I yelled. Without thinking, I grabbed

23

the lady's wrist, forcing her hand up in front of her face. "What do you know of work?" I asked her. "You with your soft, white hands!"

It was this that made her scream. An angry tirade of sounds and noises left her throat. Most of it was meaningless to me, but there was one word she repeated over and over again. "Bolshevik... Bolshevik... Bolshevik," she kept calling, writhing and kicking me as her abuse continued. Her uproar brought one of the ship's officers over in our direction, followed by a number of his men. They pulled me away from her, pinning me against a cabin wall.

This wasn't the end of it. Within moments, I was being dragged down to the captain's quarters. There I was greeted by an endless series of accusations; that I was a Bolshevik, an assassin brought on board to kill the aristocrats in the ship's company, that I had grabbed her breast, made threats towards her, tried to steal her money... To each of these claims, I said nothing. My English had deserted me. Even when I tried to think, it was Gaelic that tumbled into my head – the desperate prayers my father used to say as he knelt before his fireside chair. "A Dhia... Dhia... Thoir cuideachadh dhomh."

And there was no answer. The Almighty seemed unable to send even words that might guide my tongue – English words that I could use to defend myself against the multitude of accusations she was making. All I was able to do was listen to the Latvian woman sitting by her mother piling one fantastical claim on top of another. There was no response – not even to the ship's captain who kept urging me to speak.

"Say something, lad! Is it true what she's saying? Has the sea got your tongue?"

In the end, I was lucky. The hysterical nature of her accusations made every word that came from her lips incredible. It beggared anyone's belief that the Bolshveiks would choose a young Hebridean exile to act as an assassin for their cause; even more that they would pick a Latvian estate owner's daughter for their victim. As for the idea that the girl had been sexually molested, the captain dismissed the whole notion with a contemptuous snort.

"That young lad can't even remember where his tongue is. You can't expect him to recall the whereabouts of anything else."

With that, he waved his hand and told me to go. "And make damn sure you don't bother me again!" he shouted as I headed out the door.

I didn't. For the rest of the voyage, I spent my time with my fellow Hebrideans, singing their songs of exile – "Soraidh leis an àite..." – and joining in their psalms – "Is e Dia fèin a's buachaill dhomh…" And when I finally reached the shores of Canada, these words had become a comfort to me. They are still – a continual reminder of the people from which I came.

Baleen

It was my wee fellow, Alec, who charged into my bedroom that morning, his voice booming through my sleep.

"Dad! Dad! There's whales on the beach! Let's go down and see them!"

"Hell..." I peered out of my bedclothes, seeing the small, dark figure of my son standing at the foot of my bed. "You sure about that?"

"Yeah! There's lots of folk going to see them. Come on or we'll be the last!"

Wracked by a hangover, I padded to the window. From there, I could see a crowd gathering – all making their way to these strange black shapes that had suddenly appeared in the middle of the night. To begin with, I thought they were only rocks stripped of sand, but the way one of them moved changed my mind. They were whales all right.

"Come on... Come on," Alec urged.

"All right," I said, knowing I would have to give in to him sooner or later. After all, the lad was only with me for a couple of days and there was no doubt he was owed a little spoiling. "I'll be down in a minute."

"Great!" he yelled as he headed down to his Gran in the kitchen.

I had one eye on the road outside as I buttoned my shirt. There were a lot of folk making their way through the village of Ardale to the beach – some driving and others walking. It wasn't the first time this week there had been a scene like this. The other day they had buried my old friend and neighbour, Hector Maclean, in the nearby cemetery. Over the past year or two, we had shared many a bottle – his huge, round figure lapping over the edges of his armchair as we sat on opposite sides of the fireplace, our whisky glasses in our hands.

"You know, Peter," he said once, "what the folk of the north end of this island used to do when they thought the seas were against them? One of them would wade out into the ocean and pour a huge cup of ale into the waves. He'd say a prayer then to the sea-god Shonny, to make the seas turn good for them again."

And the two of us had smiled, wondering what our local minister would say if he ever saw any of us doing the likes of that. Hector imitated his sermon to perfection, mimicking the thin, reedy voice, the intensity of the stare, the pounding of his fist on the edge of the pulpit...

I felt glad to be in his company – the whisky and laughter numbing me against the troubles that, through luck or design, threatened to knock away the feet from under me. There was the way the boat I owned back then – the *Baleen* – seemed only to catch fish that were pocked with sores and ulcers. Or else the ones we caught were small and useless – the leavings of some East Coast trawler. A short time in Hector's company, however, and all thought of these things were gone – drained away with the bottles of whisky we had gone through together.

But even that small comfort had vanished now. Hector was dead and the *Baleen* sold to a man from Killybegs in County Donegal. And Moira...? I tried not to think of her – my son's face the only way her features forced themselves into my mind. Once again, they were there to remind me as I stepped inside the kitchen, her dark, quick eyes before me as Alec's head bobbed up from the pages of the comic he had been reading.

"You're ready?" he asked.

I nodded.

"Great!" he yelled, pulling the hood of his anorak over his dark, curly head as he made his way out the door.

He was the one who did most of the talking as we went down the road – an eight year old walking encyclopaedia on the nature and variety of whales. From the beluga to the narwhal, he knew something of them all.

"I wonder what type these are," he kept asking.

And then he had the chance to answer his question. They were there in front of us, lying on the edge of the village graveyard. It was as if the cliffs on either side of the bay had trapped the five of them on the beach; their breath only a slow, wet whistle, much too weak to think of escape. People stood around them with their hands in their pockets, watching as their huge tails flapped hopelessly on the sand. One or two even went up to them, slapping their sides to get the "feel" of blubber. Someone flashed his camera in the direction of an eye.

"I think they're pilot whales, Dad," he announced.

I nodded. My friend, Dan was making his way towards me, his face tired and grizzled from last night's session in the hotel. He nodded towards the bodies.

"Looks like the flaming plagues of Egypt," he said, taking a half-bottle from his anorak pocket. "Here. Take a swig of this. It'll cure your problems."

I accepted his offer, barely noticing Alec moving away as I raised the

27

whisky to my lips. There was something else going on at the other end of the beach. Some of the lads from the district had lifted a large piece of driftwood from the shore, heading in the direction of one of the whales. They were just about to drop it on the creature's tail when a shout rang out.

"Stop bloody doing that!"

We all looked to see from where the voice had come. It was Hennessy the vet. A round portly figure dressed in a yellow oilskin coat and the dark leggings of a diving suit, he was standing in front of the whale they had been attempting to pin down, his arms outstretched like a traffic cop. As they let the timber go, he began to lecture them, his finger wagging in their direction.

"How can you cretins do that? To a dying beast? It doesn't need you clowns to add to its misery!"

One of the boys mumbled an apology, but this didn't stop his flow.

"There's two of these creatures still alive!" he yelled. "And in a wee while, we might need you idiots to help carry them back to the water. But in the meantime, do you think you could use your muscles in a more helpful way? By keeping these creatures' bodies wet. Do you think you could manage that?"

All around the beach, people looked at each other – surprising themselves by volunteering a moment or so later.

"Great!" he grinned. "Now get yourselves busy. Get pails, coke bottles, anything – just keep these creatures wet till we can get some tarpaulins over from town. Okay?"

A few minutes later, I was among the many who were striding back and forth from the waves with tin buckets in our hands. Dan and some other fellow were tugging an old zinc bath between them. One of the village women, Mairi, had dragged out her council wheelie bin and was shoving that across the beach. And Alec was by my side, clutching large bottles of Quosh and Robinson's Barley Water. An endless set of questions were on his lips as he tried to keep pace with me, stumbling on the sand.

"Is this the first time a whale's landed here? Did you ever see one before? Did any ever frighten you?"

I tried my best to answer these last questions. "Aye. I've seen whales a couple of times before. But it was the day I never seen one that frightened me the most."

He stared at me while I dipped my bucket in the sea.

"What do you mean, Dad?"

I told him about one time when I was just out of school and working on my first fishing boat. We were barely out of harbour and the sea was as still and quiet as the waters of a loch. Then suddenly, there was a whale nearby. A spout of water showed me that. A moment or two later, there was its tail. I didn't see it, but when this wave rocked the boat, I knew it was there – close by and breaking the surface of the ocean. I held my breath for a long time, wondering if the next time it might strike against the boat.

"No wonder you were scared," Alec said.

"Aye... I was terrified." I pitched my bucket high as I said this, watching the gleam of water on the whale's back. "It was the longest minute of my life."

But that wasn't really the truth. There had been another moment when I thought I was in command of things, and then there was this sudden movement under my feet, my whole world shifting. I had come home one afternoon after some problem had started in the *Baleen*'s engines. Moira was at the washing line and I went into the kitchen to make a cup of tea for myself. It was then – lying on the kitchen table – that I found a clutch of brown envelopes. I shuffled through them, reading each one with an increasing sense of horror. There was a demand from the Hydro Electric, printed in red; a bill from a local shopkeeper; a final warning from a catalogue firm.

It was then that Moira walked in, and – for the first time in my life – I hit her, pounding my fists and feet against her time and time again.

"You stupid, stupid cow!" I was yelling. "How the hell did you let this happen? How the hell could you...?"

It was one of these moments when boundaries are crossed, when all the years and hopes and love that tied two people together are snapped away and you become like a pair of animals who have come across each other on a village road – each one distrustful and unforgiving, anxious only to wound. I trembled as I dipped my bucket in the sea again, trying to block out my memory of that day, but it was only Hennessy's voice that helped me do this. He was yelling as he stood beside one of the whales.

"We've got the tarpaulin now! Are you cretins going to help me?"

We all rushed in his direction, trying to shove the whale on top of the thick canvas sheeting. Its tail twisted as we did this, lashing out in our direction.

"Doesn't the devil know we're trying to save it?" Dan asked, his face clenched as he tried to keep a hold.

Clearly it didn't. As we carried it to the sea, its writhing reminded me of the times the *Baleen*'s nets had been full – the wriggling of fish, their desperate flurries at escape making us smile as we hauled them in. There was the same spirit about this venture. We were grinning even as we stumbled –

our footsteps slithering on the seaweed rotting on the beach.

A moment later we were in the water, our bodies chilled by the waves. Dan was muttering something about wanting to "postpone his cross-Channel swim", when Hennessy looked over, nodding to the man on the other side of the tarpaulin.

"All right... Let flicking go."

An instant later, the whale was in the water, and we were rushing out. I ran back to the shore to find Alec by my side. He was bouncing up and down, shouting with excitement as the whale headed out of the bay.

"Do you think it'll do it, Dad?" His hand reached out to mine. "Do you think it'll be all right?"

But his fingers slipped away when it became clear it wouldn't. The whale was moving slowly, looking as though it were unwilling to leave the shelter of the shoreline, and then it stopped altogether. Its strength seemed to give out as it went farther – slowed down by the force of each incoming breaker. And then it was Dan who was standing beside me, offering me the comfort of his half-bottle.

"Put that down you before we get the other one," he said.

Yet that was the same story. Within the hour, both whales were lying trapped on the rocks at the side of the bay, the tide the only pulse that moved their bodies. The other three lay alongside the graveyard fence – like hearses in attendance at some tragedy. Alec was lying crouched beside one when I went to take him home. His face was smeared with sand and tears as he looked up at me.

"Why does everything have to go wrong?" he asked.

I was back there that evening. Dan and I had gone for a few drinks at the hotel – trying to chase away the misery we shared – and now we were once again on the beach, sitting in his car. The only noises we could hear were the slap of the windscreen wipers, the dark heave of the sea, and the occasional smack of lips and sound of swallowing as we raised our cans and bottles to our lips.

"What made those whales come here?" I asked for the hundredth time that night.

Dan took a swig from his half-bottle, responding with the same answer I had heard a hundred times before. "Hell knows... No one knows... No one knows for certain."

But some people had tried to guess. Lifting my bottle to my lips, I struggled to make sense of their suggestions – to give some sort of explanation for the whales' presence on the shore. Someone had said that the bay had an orange sheen the previous day; evidence of some chemical or other killing them. Or maybe the whale's navigational system had gone wrong – the beasts trapped on the beach by mistake. But it was another notion that appealed to me – the idea Hennessy had spoken about in the bar – that if one member of a whale family beached itself to die, the others followed in its wake, unwilling to be parted from their kin.

I swallowed my whisky, wishing we humans were made that way. Instead, when troubles came to a family, we scattered left and right – unable to stand together. The last year had shown me that. There was the *Baleen* sailing different waters; Moira struggling to bring up the wee fellow in town; Alec's little face twisted with bitterness, washed up and alone because of our failings.

And there was Hector too… With a flick of the headlamps, I could see his final resting place. His grave would be freshly dug – still without a headstone to mark it as its own.

It was then I had the mad idea to go and see him. Stumbling out there to his grave. To offer him a drink. To have someone with whom I could share my problems. I fumbled for the door-handle in the dark.

"Where you going?" Dan muttered as I heaved my way out of the car.

I didn't answer, slamming the door shut behind me. Yet somehow, my feet didn't take me to the graveyard; its gate tied with this impossible knot. And then I was on my way. Out past the fence. Scuttling down the sandbank. And then scrambling to my feet once again. And all the time I was talking – jabbering to myself. Remembering how Hector used to tell me about how the men from the north end of the island prayed to their sea-god – what was his name? – when the ocean was against them. Well, it was certainly against us now, wasn't it? It was definitely against us these days.

And that's when an even crazier notion came into my head – to wade out into the sea and pray to the sea-god, whatever his name was. My feet stumbled as I made my way in its direction. One time I almost tripped over a plastic buoy that had been washed up there; next, my feet snarled on some fence wire.

And then when I reached the water, I raised my whisky bottle and emptied it, howling out my prayer to the sea-god. It was an endless complaint – all about dead whales and orange seas, pock-marked fish and the *Baleen*. Moira and Alec, too, were mentioned – their names an endless keening on my lips. But even in the darkness, I knew there would never be an answer.

Only the noise of the ocean as it pounded the bodies of the whales.

Ghost Dance

"Why did we come here?" Charlotte complained the day the last of her children left home. "There is nothing to keep people... Nothing... Only a stony land and a dangerous ocean."

Farquhar did not answer, surprised by the bitterness of her words. He had always been dimly aware that hidden behind what seemed to him to be her calm acceptance of her life on the island, his wife was deeply unhappy. One of a number of North American Indian women brought back from Canada in the twenties, she had for years appeared to be reconciled to the changes the move had caused in her life. After her youngest son had followed her other children to the mainland, however, her display of contentment had ended. She began to mutter resentfully about her surroundings; its high winds, the bare, treeless landscape, the sun that so rarely came to light up its skies all became the subjects of her anger. Soon it raged, too, against the native islanders, her sallow skin becoming chilled and white with fury.

"I hate those churchfolk here," she would say. "There is nothing! No colour or music in their lives!"

Farquhar would not disagree with this. He was not a religious man nor did he come from a particularly religious family. In fact, his grandfather had been one of the few men who had held onto their fiddles when the church had ordered the burning of all the musical instruments on the island. Later, he would often entertain his young grandson by telling him stories of former times, describing even the movements of many of the old dances that people had once performed on the island – dances that went under the queer titles like "The Black Sluggard" and "The Old Woman of the Quern Dust".

"In the Quern Dust dance," he would recall the old man telling him, *"the man used to have a piece of wood in his hand which he would wave at the woman, striking not far away from her head as they danced round each other, changing places again and again..."*

But for all Farquhar's dislike of the church, the vehemence of Charlotte's hatred alarmed him. It seemed to grow as the months went on, a madness that would flame in the darkness of her eyes. There was one time, for instance, when she met the minister on his walk through the village, greeting the arrival of his black-suited form by spitting on the road. Farquhar mumbled an apology for her actions, more distressed than the minister by her odd behaviour.

"What did you do that for?" he hissed.

Her face became clenched with anger. "They have done more than that to me," she said.

His nervousness in her company increased the day she came back from the well, swinging a half-empty pail of water in her hand. As she stepped into their home, he acknowledged her with a nod, but she seemed not to notice him. It was as if his features – his head with its thick covering of grey hair – were no longer familiar to her. Gesturing to the pail, he spoke:

"Why didn't you fill it?"

She didn't even glance at him in reply, but as she placed the pail on the table, he realised she was talking to herself. Her words were neither Gaelic or English, both languages she had learned. Instead, he thought her speech was nonsensical – a medley of noises without meaning – but soon he began to realise she was speaking in the Indian language she had used as a child. Startled by the strangeness of her tongue, he rose from his chair.

"What are you saying?"

There was no response; only her eyes staring, her lips a blur of sounds. A rush of panic passed through him, his voice becoming harsh and sharp.

"Charlotte. Stop it! Stop it!"

Her head jerked back as if she had been stung. Raising her hand to her mouth, she rubbed her lip as if this had been the source of the pain. Tearful, she spoke to him again, this time in English.

"I'm sorry…" she said. "I forgot."

She walked away, her head low and troubled. He looked after her sadly, convinced that this woman he had loved and taken from the shores of Canada was now losing her mind.

It was shortly after this that Farquhar realised why Charlotte had behaved in the way she did. He remembered a talk they had once had in the early years of their marriage. He had told her that when his people had gone to school, they had been punished for speaking Gaelic by having a wooden collar fixed around their necks. Only English was allowed in the classroom. She had nodded with understanding at this and then slowly, hesitantly, went on to tell a story about her own schooldays. If the missionaries who taught them found them speaking any language other than English, their punishment was even more severe. They would be made to bite down as hard as they could on a large rubber band. The missionary would than stretch this back as far as he could before letting it go – fast and hard – against their mouths. It was clearly in response to this imagined blow that Charlotte had winced, feeling the impact of that rubber band still sore upon her lip some sixty years after the missionary had released it from his hand.

Yet there was more to her madness than the memory of past wrongs... There was a longing, too, for her former life; days when she would sit for hours upon the shoreline, as if she hoped to catch a glimpse of the Canada all these hundreds of miles away. One day she ran the length of their croft to their home, her lined face suddenly fresh and childlike with delight. She dragged out their travelling chest from its place in the bedroom, packing her clothes in a frenzy.

"I'm going!" she shouted. "I'm going home!"

Farquhar wept that night, saddened by the way he had to bring two of the village women to his home to restrain her. As he watched them battle with her, he had seen shades of the Red Indian of legend. Charlotte was whooping and screaming, her fingernails and teeth flashing. The sight had terrified him – the woman whom for years had been close to him transformed into a wild and foreign creature, as unpredictable as the ocean in her moods.

Yet lying beside her in their box-bed, watching her features soften with sleep, he could remember the many times her face had seemed to reflect his own emotions, sharing his pride when she held their first child in her arms, his sorrow when their children had left home, his joys and troubles... It was because of these experiences – the contrasting events and feelings of a lifetime spent together – that Farquhar did not want to lose her. Even though her sanity was ebbing away from her, he did not want to let her go.

Troubled in his sleep, he thought he was still dreaming when she woke him the following morning. The sullen face of the previous night had disappeared and in its place there was a new lightness. Her eyes bright with laughter, she poked her head out of the blankets, tickling the tip of his nose with an outstretched finger.

"Wake up, sleepy man!" she shouted. "It's time to rise! It's time to shine!"

He watched her when, nimble as a young girl, she leaped over his side of the bed and began to get dressed. Her fingers wrestled with her clothing; her arms and legs obstacles to overcome. Finally, she worked her way free, emerging from the snare of a heavy sweater to grin at him again.

"It's a beautiful day today," she announced.

He nodded, though halfway through dressing himself, he could hear the wind and rain roar above the roof-top. The storm rumbled across the chimney, echoing in the room below.

"Do you know what I'm going to do today?" she said. "I'm going to do that dance you told me about. The Ghost Dance... The one which Crazy Horse and his followers used to do." She veiled her eyes with her hand before stretching out her arm in a slow, rhythmic manner, chanting a series of syllables as she did so. Almost as suddenly as she began, she stopped doing this, halting her movements abruptly and turning to him for his approval. "Let us hope it will bring back the old days, the old ideas just as you always hoped it would do. Then the buffalo will return to our land, our forests and plains will be restored... Even our old songs and stories would be heard once again."

He smiled vacantly at her, wondering whom she thought he might be. He didn't know. All he could be certain of was that for the first time in months she was acting as if he were in the same room. There was interest in her eyes as she spoke to him – even if her words seemed to be those of a child addressing her father rather than those of a husband and wife. He felt an odd comfort in listening to her talk, hoping that some sense of companionship could be salvaged from the years they'd spent together.

"Come on," she said, clutching at his hand. "Watch me."

He followed her outside, watching as she stepped into the wind and rain. She skipped nimbly over a puddle, her bare feet leaving prints on the ground. It was then she began her dance, starting in much the same way as she had within her home. Her back towards him, she covered her eyes with her hand.

Then she moved her arm away, turning on her heel to face him. At the same time, she began to sing, her voice at war with the fury of the storm.

"Ah – yo – ham, ay – yo – ka – be..."

He peered at her – this alarming figure he had married. Her black hair was tangled from the wind and her eyes were wide and crazed. She performed a series of frenzied, jagged movements, toes pounding the mud, while the storm surged, making her sway from side to side. Sometimes she was poised on one foot; sometimes on the other. But at all times, her chanting continued, bringing the people of the village out from their homes to stare.

"Aw – ke – yah, far – ka – say..."

As he watched her, he felt himself long for much the same things as his wife – for the world to be restored to all it had been before, when both he and Charlotte had laughed at the antics of their children, working together side by side, sharing the labour of the field, the peat bank and the shore...

"She has returned to being a heathen," Dòmhnall the elder said, looking at Charlotte when she had been brought indoors once again. She was wearing a dry set of clothes as she sat in the corner of the room, a few strands of long hair sticking to her cheekbones. Her jaw jutting outwards, she fixed the visitors – Dòmhnall and the minister – with a hard and blazing look. They seemed to be unaware of her hostility, ostensibly there to comfort the husband they sat beside.

"No doubt there was always a danger of that happening," the minister said, swallowing a mouthful of tea. "What's bred in the bone often comes out in the flesh. Our church has seen that so many times in its work in Africa. For every one saved, there are ten who adhere to their old gods."

Farquhar stared outwards, barely listening to a word his companions said. He was studying Charlotte again, watching how a shy little smile often played on the corners of her face. Looking at her, he could often glimpse the child she had been years ago – the child she had once more been today. Whom had she imagined him to be earlier? Her father? Her grandfather? Most likely, the latter. He imagined him to be an old white-haired man much like his own, sitting her on his knee while he explained the legends and dances of his people, detailing every move their ancient tribesmen had made...

"Why do you think that happens?" the elder asked, interrupting his thoughts.

The minister sighed, his feet outstretched on the clay floor. "I don't know," he declared. "They claim to be Christians for a few years and then they slide back into their old ways, returning to the gods they left behind. These tribal gods bear no resemblance to the Christian one. They could be the ones whom they feel rule the crops and the seasons. Even their dead ancestors. It is to them that they finally give their loyalty..."

Half-hearing this, Farquhar remembered the stories told by his grandfather. He had explained why the people of the area had performed the dance they called "The Old Woman of the Quern Dust". It had been a corn-dance; one supposed to guarantee that both the crops and man himself would be restored the following spring. The Old Woman would be struck down and then be brought back to life a short time later – like the seeds from last year's harvest scattered on the earth the following spring. Farquhar could recall, too, the directions he had been given.

"The man used to have a piece of wood in his hand which he would wave at the woman, striking not far away from her head as they danced round each other, changing places again and again..."

Slowly, he rose from his chair, the conversation of the two men stilling as he did so. Charlotte smiled as he walked towards her, her friendly, open

36

greeting resembling that of a guileless child. She stretched out her hand towards him and he covered it with his own, marvelling at the way her lined and tired face still retained the freshness of childhood, a sense that the passing of time had not occurred. Yet he knew, too, that if he did not find some way of reaching her, it would not be long before she would be beyond his grasp – as remote as any stranger.

It was then he had an idea. He would teach her how to perform the dances of his own people. She would no longer then retreat into a past that was foreign to him – one that belonged to another, different world. With this in mind, he smiled kindly at her, clutching her hand more firmly.

"Can I teach you some new dances?" he said.

And she grinned eagerly in response, looking at him with a love and affection he had not seen since the early days of their marriage. She wrapped her arms around him, hugging him closely to her chest.

"I would love you to do that," she said.

Gifts from Abroad

Before that Monday we had only used our tongues against Duncan, tormenting him and calling him names. This time, however, we felt a new righteous bitterness – one that expressed itself in the fury of our fists and feet as he lay in the background.

"You liar!" I hissed at him. "You dirty filthy liar!"

Duncan looked at me in desperation – dirt clinging to his face, hot and sticky with tears and sweat. "I'm not..." he muttered. "Mum told me these things... They're all true..."

There was only one reaction to his denial. Another kick. This time it came from RD's direction. Duncan winced as his toe drove hard into his ribs. He rolled over, his back towards RD as his tormentor began to speak.

"No. They're not! Dad told me. They're all lies! All flaming stupid lies! You haven't got a father. He vanished years ago. The sod didn't even wait around long enough to marry your Ma."

"But my Dad writes these letters..."

"No! He doesn't!" It was my turn to yell. "That's nonsense! All your flipping imagination!"

"No. No. No. You're all wrong." And this time it was Duncan's hand that moved, fumbling in his jacket pocket. He scrambled there for a long time. When his fingers emerged, they were clutching some pieces of wood. For all that it was tight within his grip, it was possible to make out the shape of the object he was holding. There was a large head adorned with an ornate head-dress; a carefully carved torso; a set of overlong arms and legs – one of which had been clearly broken in the fight. On each limb, a tiny wooden pole was fastened, hanging like a stilt.

"There," he smiled, his eyes bright with tears. "What did I tell you? He sent me that. My Dad sent me that."

We were all silent as we looked down upon the smashed fragments in his hand. All we could remember were the events of the previous day when he had been with the rest of us on the shoreline. We could recall the stories he had told – the tales that had been mocked and contradicted by our parents later that evening. These wooden pieces – delicate and finely carved – added

38

to our bemusement, forcing us to question our mothers' and fathers' words. It was because of them that we all stood motionless, wondering whether to deliver yet another blow, or to allow him to rise once again to his feet...

He had found us where we always headed on a Sunday, walking to a small beach that was sheltered on one side by the slope of a hill, the other by a cliff. We went there each week to claim possession of it, playing a game which, if it was ever discovered by the stern churchmen in the district, would be frowned on and condemned. Somehow, too, it was also our "sea" that lapped against it, one which we shared with other countries, like Canada and the States to the west and the Scandinavian nations to our north and east. It thrilled us that many of our fathers knew these places; the majority having been – or still were – sailors in the Merchant Navy.

It was not a part of our experience that Duncan shared. None of us had ever thought to ask where his father was. We only knew that he lived with his mother in a small cottage near the centre of the village. For this and many other reasons, we didn't like him near us. RD made this clear when he approached, clutching his nose and muttering:

"Here comes the tink. He makes a right old stink..."

Yet Duncan continued to tag along as we walked along the shoreline, stopping with us too, when we talked with some older men whom we met upon our way. They gathered in the same place every Sunday, resting on the summit of a hill a few hundred yards from our beach. They would sit on the cropped machair grass for ages, spending much of the Sabbath rolling their own fags or lying with the waistbands of their trousers unbuttoned after their afternoon meal. There was Symie, his chill-blue eyes continually scanning the coastline, a long blade of grass clamped between his teeth; Malkie Gunn with his gnarled and serious face at odds with the cloth cap that was twisted comically back to front on his head; Mac with his series of nervous tics and gestures, brandishing his arms every time he spoke... And the words that were on their lips? These were invariably place-names – ones like "Durban"; "Sydney"; "Montreal"; "San Francisco". The mention of each of these cities pulled us to a sea-borne life with the same force and rigour as the tide that tugged the ocean only a short distance away.

Today it was Malkie's turn to talk. His face grew even more shadowed than normal as he spoke of working on the supply boats sailing to Stavanger in Norway during the Second World War. "Jeez," he would say, "it was the most bitter wind I've ever felt in all my days. One moment you'd have a cup of hot tea tight within your mitt and the next you could see the ice form on it.

There'd be frost all over your whiskers as you choked the thing down."

As his words faltered and halted, we felt once again our awe at the power of the sea, silenced by its mights. This was a sensation shared by all of us – even Duncan. I could see his eyes were bright; his mouth hanging open, revealing a set of teeth in which a number were either black or missing.

"And where's your father just now?" Symie's question – directed at me – brought an end to our silence. "Still in South America?"

I nodded. "We got a letter from him last week. He's in Rio at the moment."

"Rio." Symie puckered his lips. "Now that's a place I've never been." He tugged a blade of grass out of the earth and wound it like a wedding ring round one of his fingers. "No. The only parts of South America I've been to were the Panama Canal and Nicaragua. Poor places they both were. Any of the rest of you ever been anywhere in that direction?"

Mac waved his arm, acting as if the whole of South America was well within his reach. "A-a-a-argentina and the F-f-f-falkland Islands," he stuttered.

"I've been in Valaparaiso in Chile," Malkie added, taking a long breath...

It was clear he was just about to begin a story when he was interrupted. Duncan's voice – alive and trembling with excitement – burst into the conversation. There was no halting the rush of words that came to his lips.

"My Dad's in Singapore at the moment. He's been in the Orient a long time. Says it's his favourite place in the world."

After he had spoken, there was silence – one that was broken by the "kleep" of an oyster-catcher as it flew overhead. Its long orange beak gave it much of the appearance of a winged clown – the only creature that dared to jeer at Duncan's sudden and unexpected remark. The men, on the other hand, only looked confused. Symie cast a quizzical glance in Malkie's direction. The other man answered this with a bewildered shrug. Meanwhile, Mac looked even more agitated than usual, his mouth opening and closing in astonishment.

"I didn't know that," Malkie finally said.

"Oh... yes." Wide-eyed and breathless, Duncan was pleased to have joined the conversation. "Mum says he'll be back home next year if things go reasonably well."

Symie sucked in a mouthful of smoke, weighing up every word that came from this lad's lips. It was clear that neither he – nor anyone else – knew how to react to them; this reference to a man no one could ever recall seeing. "That's good, Duncan," he muttered. "I hope you won't have to wait long."

Yet even after he had spoken, the silence and awkwardness of the group seemed to linger. There was a stiffness about the way we all reacted to one another – a series of irritated coughs and sighs; a twitching and shifting as we sat there on the ground. It was finally ended when Malkie leaned over to whisper to RD. The old man's face was dark and troubled as he spoke.

"Isn't it about time you young fellows went away by yourselves for a while?"

There it was – the dismissal. It was the first time it had ever happened after such a short while in their company. Normally, they were only too content to have us there an audience for all their stories – and it was our own restlessness, our urge to play football that pulled us to our feet. This time, we left reluctantly, aware that Duncan's presence had disturbed their rest.

We tried to shake off this feeling, rushing to the beach. Our football was waiting for us there, smuggled to the shoreline the evening before. We gathered it from its hiding place – the front entrance to a rabbit burrow where RD had left it wedged and scurried down the hillside to the sand below. When we arrived there, Alasdair kicked in the air. The moment it touched the ground again, RD yelled: "Give it to me!"

I was the nearest, kicking it in his direction. RD grabbed it, holding it in his hands as he advanced towards Duncan. A few feet away and he threw it against the lad's chest. Duncan doubled up, coughing as some grains of sand caught within his throat. He looked up at his attacker.

"You're telling the truth about your dad?" RD questioned.

"Yes," Duncan brushed away the sand that had clustered on his lips.

RD picked up the ball again, throwing it hard against Duncan's face. "How come we've never heard of him before?"

. Duncan's mouth quivered. "Oh… that's because he's been away for years. Before he arrived in Singapore, he spent some time working on the west coastline of Africa – countries like Sierra Leone and Liberia. Before then he lived in a few other countries. Papua New Guinea, Taiwan, Indonesia… he helps all these governments organise their navies and ports. That's why he spent the last nine years away. He's so much in demand."

We greeted this litany of place-names with a mixture of disbelief and astonishment. Sierra Leone, Liberia, Papua New Guinea, Taiwan, Indonesia… every name seemed so fresh and startling, exotic among the familiar shades with which our maps of the worlds were coloured – the "Durbans", "Sydneys" and "Montreals" we had heard about so often. Each unusual location sparkled and caught our attention, blurring many of the doubts we held about this man's existence. It was only RD who retained his former scepticism, growling out another question.

"You mean to say he hasn't been back in all that time."

"No... He'd love to though. Mum always reads his letters and he keeps on saying how he'd love to be home. Once or twice he's nearly made it, but something always prevents him. The last time was while he was in Indonesia and some civil war broke out. The government had to keep him there as one of the advisers to their navy."

Duncan said all this with such conviction I couldn't help half-believing him. It was easy to picture the scene in his home every time a letter arrived. There would be his mother's smile of hope when the postman arrived with an envelope, its right hand corner covered with a colourful array of foreign stamps. She would open this with shaking fingers, her face becoming troubled as she read the message it contained. Her husband would be delayed again, caught up in some troubles in the country where he was based. Duncan would share her disappointment when later that evening she would read its words aloud, wondering if there would ever come a day when he would see his father again. Even RD's features softened as he listened to Duncan talk, perhaps picturing all this in his mind.

"Tell us about some other places he's been to then," he asked.

And Duncan answered, conjuring a new strange planet with his words. It was one where familiar places had been cast into shadow and new and unusual locations brought out into the light. There was the heat and humidity of West Africa, apparently the venue of a tribal dance celebrated in honour of his father's birthday. Through the spell wrought by his speech, we could hear the beat of the drum, catch sight of their colourful head-dresses and costumes – our hearts and minds under his sway. From there, we were taken to the forests of Papua New Guinea. There was no welcoming tribe to be found there – only the savagery of spears pointed in his father's direction, their shafts swaying in the hands of a group of natives who greeted him in the jungle. He only managed to escape because a troop of soldiers appeared, their bullets more deadly than the sharpened tips of tribal weapons.

"And what about these other places he went to?" RD's voice was quiet as he asked the question.

It was then Duncan mentioned the shadow-puppets he had received from his father. They had come from Indonesia and were used in ceremonial displays and dances, re-enactments of some of the folk-tales of their culture. It seemed that their silhouettes moved rhythmically across well-lit screens, cast in their roles as native gods and heroes. The music of the local people marched in harmony with their every move. "I'll bring it into school tomorrow," he announced. "You can all see it then."

We nodded as he said this, desperate to see the evidence that would confirm us in our beliefs. "Aye. You do that... We'd love to look at it."

It was this – the final proof of his father's existence – that now lay broken in Duncan's hand. Still, he continued to proffer it to us. A flimsy and disjointed figure, it was impossible to imagine it performing anything but the most frenzied movements to music. Measured against our parents' words, it seemed a pitiful object – confirmation that Duncan's father was a piece of fiction as fanciful as any of his tales.

"You expect us to believe you?" RD grunted.

The figure was not withdrawn. It still hung loosely from his hands. RD snatched it from him, tossing it onto the ground. He smashed it under his heel – the little smile on the puppet's face growing wider as his shoe pounded down again and again, splitting his head in two.

"You'd better face something," he muttered. "Your dad left a long time ago, long before you were born. And who could blame him? He must have had a good idea how you'd turn out."

And this time it was my boot that struck him. I can recall the impact on his arm as my foot slammed against his body – the scream that escaped his bleeding mouth. As we walked away from him, I felt an odd satisfaction, as if the pain we had inflicted on his dirty, shivering form had been justified by his own actions. He was the evil one, the false-mouthed figure who had tricked and fooled us with his lies.

The Coming of English

On the first Thursday in November, a telegram arrived at Chrissie's home.

Using her thumb-nail as a knife, she tore its envelope open and took the piece of paper out. She did not try to read the words that were written there. They were printed in English, a language she had never been taught. For a short time, she stared at them, cursing the lack of knowledge which prevented her from understanding the meaning of the words. Finally, she folded it away and placed it behind the tilly-lamp on the dresser. She would have to ask the local headmaster to read it to her later.

In the meantime, she decided to forget about it, pretending to herself it had never been received. There was work to be done. The sheep still had to be fed. The cow remained to be milked and cared for. Her son had gone away to the war which had recently started and the whole burden of the croft rested on her shoulders. Yet she never wasted any time complaining about this. She gave her work more attention and energy than she would ever have expected from anybody else.

When she had finally completed all the tasks she had set herself to do, she picked up the telegram in her hand and set off in the direction of the schoolhouse. There were others in the village who could read and understand English but she always took any letter she received along to the headmaster. There was a coldness and distance about him which was lacking in her fellow villagers. With them, she could never be certain that her information would not be spread about the district, speeded by their quick and gossiping tongues. As she hurried along, she crumpled the envelope between her fingers, believing it contained some welcome news about her son.

She knocked at the schoolhouse door, granting the house a respect she never gave to any other in the district. For a few moments she stood anxiously on the door-step. It was then the headmaster appeared. He was a grim-featured man, not given to warmth but his dark face lightened when he saw her.

"Good day, Chrissie. It's good to see you... How are you keeping these days?"

"I'm fine, Headmaster... and you?"

"Grand."

He smiled in reply, gesturing to the open door. She followed him in, the warm scent of the peat-fire filling her lungs as she entered the sitting room. She always felt slightly awkward while she was there. The headmaster's wife kept a beautiful home. Its fine leather chairs glinted in the firelight. There were books stretched across one wall. She glanced at one that lay open on the fireside table, blind to the meaning of its words. The whole place seemed a world away from the darkness and damp of her own thatched cottage.

"Would you like a cup of tea?" the headmaster smiled.

"No... no," she answered, waving her hand to emphasise her refusal. "I just came along to ask you to read this for me."

She held out the crumpled envelope between her fingers. The headmaster took it from her, withdrawing the piece of paper from its folds. He smiled cheerfully.

"It's a telegram," he said.

The headmaster began to read it. As his eyes moved along the line, his face darkened, filling up with fear and doubt. He looked at her with sadness in his eyes.

"Sit down, Chrissie."

She obeyed him slowly, struggling to read his thoughts from his voice. The headmaster smoothed a hair back from his forehead.

"Your son's been killed."

She said nothing, staring at the fire before her. He took his handkerchief from his pocket and wiped his brow. He was unsure whether or not his words had been understood.

"I'm sorry... but John won't be returning from the war."

Death is always strange. She remembered the day her husband died. When the last sound had escaped him, she had continued to search his long familiar face for signs of life, swearing she could feel the warmth of his breath on her fingers. It seemed stranger still today. Trapped on a piece of paper, written in an unknown foreign tongue, it was somehow less real than it might otherwise have been. She shook her head and turned angrily towards the headmaster.

"Is that the way they tell people? A piece of paper... A language that few here can understand... Is that how they tell a mother that her son is dead?"

The headmaster shrugged his shoulders hopelessly, searching for the right reply.

She stood up. As she did so, a single tear fell down her cheek. She brushed it away angrily with the back of her hand. She would not cry here.

In a room full of English books, her mourning would seem odd and out of place. Instead, she would return home. Her tears would fall freely there, untroubled by the language which had come to bring her death.

Murdag

With every year another piece of the black felt that covered her roof would tear loose, flapping and rattling each night as Murdag tried to sleep, but she would never think of replacing it. Instead, she would ask one of the village men to nail this section down, ignoring the way they all claimed the fabric had rotted, its underside worn and damp.

"It did for my father," she would mutter. "It'll do for me till I'm gone."

She was like that, too, with the rest of the house, preserving it as it had been while her father was alive. The fact that she had to go for water to a standing pipe at the end of the house "would do" for her. So, too, would the tilly-lamp that lit each room. She had never allowed electricity to be wired inside her home. People would misunderstand all this, blaming Murdag's meanness for the absence of a fridge or phone, yet when anyone came to her door, she was generous enough, putting money in their collecting cans for the lifeboat or the starving children in Africa, giving help when it was needed by a neighbour.

It wasn't a lack of generosity that made her act this way. It was her reverence for her father, Uisdean, whose portrait hung above the fireplace in her sitting room. With his black suit, white moustache, dark eyes that glared outwards with authority, he appeared to have the clenched and frozen stance that was shared by most fathers of his generation. "Honour thy father" he seemed to command. It would be a brave soul that would dare to defy him.

Yet images deceive. Appearances can play the fool. Looking at him from her fireside chair, Murdag could remember a man that was full of love, see a flicker of affection in eyes where most folk could only witness harshness and strength. She could recall too how, as a girl of nineteen, she had worked with her gutting knife in the herring fishing in Wick. While her head was bowed over barrels filled with fish, a young fisherman from Buckie had approached her. With his easy manner, his compliments for the fineness of her form and her long red hair, he had coaxed her into bed. Pregnant from that encounter, she had returned home to meet her mother's anger. For days there was the same quarrel; the same set of words spoken in new and ever more spiteful ways.

"Can you hear the rest of the village talking about you? You will suffer for this for the rest of your life…"

Nursing a stomach full of bitterness it was easy for Murdag to picture the village-folk talking about her. Night after night her sleep was disturbed by the echo of their tongues. She could hear each "tut" of disapproval, the stern puckering of their lips, the admonitions to their daughters: "Make sure you don't go the same way." Only her father seemed quiet and calm, his thoughts as hard to grasp as the smoke that clouded from his pipe. Yet even from a glance, Murdag could see he was doing his utmost to control his temper. His foot beat an angry rhythm on the floor when she stood before him. His heavy sighs meant he was ashamed of her; each one an unspoken wish that she had never been born.

At the same time, however, he was the one that produced the first gesture of kindness towards her. A month or so before the child was due, he walked up to her, carrying a cradle in his hands. It had been made by his own fingers, using the carpenter's skills he had practised for years.

"For the child," he said shyly as he gave it to her.

Murdag took it gratefully, accepting it as a sign that his anger had calmed. He was reconciled now to the arrival of the child she would bear…

It was the first tentative sign of the love he would afterwards display proudly. When her son was born, he took the child in his arms and smiled broadly – his feet light and lively as he moved around the blackhouse floor.

"Murdo…" he said. "Can we call the boy Murdo?"

She nodded, knowing it was his father's name: one that had been in his family for generations. Her own name, Murdag, was in itself derived from it, an expression of her father's longing for a son. There were times when she resented this. The choice seemed in some ways a denial of her sex; the hard "g" that was its final consonant a blunt and ugly sound, but all these things made little difference now. She reached once again for Murdo, embracing him in her arms. The child had claims upon her. The warmth of his flesh, the clenching of his little fists nudged and coaxed her from the isolation she had chosen over the past few months. His fretful crying muffled the other sounds that went on around her – the voices that would condemn her for the mistake she had made while away from the protection of her home.

"She shows no shame, does she? You'd think she was almost proud of what she did. She would be better off looking for the child's father."

For years the sharpness of such words hurt her. She would leave the fireside when most folk entered, going out to one of the other rooms in the house. Yet as time went on, she developed some protection against their

48

comments – a shell of hard skin forming over the wounds their tongues made. She found much of her strength in watching the affection which her father showed to Murdo. The boy followed the older man everywhere, sitting on his knee when the men of the village met and talked, or tumbling in his footsteps when he went off to tend some crop or animal on his croft. Uisdean would also show the lad how to master the art of carpentry, teaching him how to hammer a nail straight or plane a stretch of wood to a perfect smoothness. Murdo would rejoice in all this, relishing each moment he spent with his grandfather.

It was Uisdean's visits to "Grundy" – the local butcher – that Murdo enjoyed more than anything else. The man had bought the first van in the village, driving down the roads of the district with his meat displayed on hooks and shelves behind him. It was a position young Murdo loved to occupy. Sitting in the driver's seat, he would turn the wheel round each narrow corner, sounding the horn to send sheep and hens scattering before him. His enthusiasm was not shared by Uisdean. The older man would shake his head when he was offered a ride in the van, distrusting the vehicle his friend had bought.

"I'll stay on my own two feet," he would laugh. "If I stepped on board, I'd soon be as dead as all those chops you carry. I have an idea that's where you get them from. Pieces of those poor folk that come to buy your meat."

He would guffaw when he said this, pretending he was not entirely serious, but one glance at his pale and wan face was more than enough to show he felt more than a little wary of this new form of transport. It would take a great deal of effort to persuade him to step anywhere near it.

Yet for all his dislike of modern mechanics, there were times when Uisdean displayed some interest in his future. It was a characteristic that seemed to grow along with Murdo – the boy's arrival stirring him into a new restlessness, an unwillingness to accept his own ageing. He planned and dreamed continually, wanting to build a new home instead of the thatched house where they had lived since their marriage. When he first mentioned this, his wife objected, waving her hand contemptuously to try and dismiss his strange ambitions.

"Where are we going to get the money from? At our time of life, do we want change?"

His campaign continued – week after week of relentless persuasion. "We've got to think of Murdag and the boy," he would say. "They need something better than this."

Finally, she relented, turning towards him with a weary expression on her face. "All right," she sighed. "Have it your own way."

He began then to build...

There were two floors to this new home, much higher then the traditional "black house" that lay flat and squat before the island's winds. Night after night, Uisdean worked upon it, hoisting stones to make its walls, constructing "storm windows" on its upstairs floor. The village folk would listen to him hammering in the darkness; the screech of his saw competing with the squealing of cats when night-time fell. Their only response was to mock and jeer his efforts.

"A storm will soon topple a giant like that... Old Uisdean's getting above himself – in more ways than one."

Yet if Murdag ever heard them, she would have dismissed their words, blaming them on resentment and envy. As Uisdean continued working with Murdo at his side, she was content to remain in the old blackhouse with no-one but her mother for company. She could see from their doorway their new home taking shape: its walls gaining height, the roof-beams set in place, the black felt later covering them. A short time later, she was working there too; wielding a paint-brush on its walls and staircase, brushing its floors clean, helping to carry their furniture from the black house to their new surroundings. As each stage passed, she felt more and more at peace with herself. The building of the house had given her a sense of her own worth – a self-esteem she had lost the day she found she was pregnant with Murdo.

It was while she was standing at an upstairs window, hanging a set of curtains she had bought, that she realised this. Down on the ground, she could see two village-women talking, nodding their heads in occasional agreement with each other, shrugging their shoulders when they were uncertain over some point. At that moment it seemed to Murdag that they were small and insignificant creatures, their voices too low and hushed to ever reach the point at which she now stood.

She laughed then. For too long, she had felt their words mattered, recalling how they had echoed in her bedroom all those years before. Now they no longer disturbed her. Going downstairs, she had rushed to her father, clutching him in her arms. He had laughed when this happened, embarrassed by her show of affection.

"What on earth's up with you?" he had asked.

And she had been unable to answer, choked by the tears that threatened to overwhelm her, deprived of a voice that might tell of the gratitude she felt.

It was with these feelings of warmth and closeness that the years went past. She measured the progress of time in the changes that had had taken place in his son – now in his young manhood – and the lines etched both on her own face and those of others she knew. Her mother's death occurred too, but the loss of her voice – for years grumbling in a corner – made little difference to her life. She was more troubled by her father's faltering pace. His hands had become slow and arthritic; his breath a laboured wheeze that barely took him through each day. There were times when she would watch him seethe with impatience at his clumsiness; the awkward, stumbling way in which he would attempt the simplest tasks.

But when Murdo came home, tired after finishing a day's work, Uisdean's face would lighten, anxious to find out what was happening on the island. He had helped to buy his grandson a lorry, purchasing this when it became clear the lad had no real interest in working with wood for the rest of his life. Engines, however, fascinated him. The lad was more at ease holding a driving wheel than a hammer. In a short time, it was his vehicle that took most of the timber and cement from town, bringing it to the village where it was used to build the new "white houses" that were being constructed all around the district; many of them the work of those who had mocked and jeered Uisdean when he had laboured on his own home a number of years before... But it was not these cargoes in which Uisdean showed any interest when Murdo returned home each evening. Instead, it was the tales the young man carried in his head; the rumours, news and scandals people spoke about in the island.

"Anything new in the town today? Hear anything interesting over there?" he would ask.

Murdag would barely listen as her son replied, almost mindless in the shuttle back and forth of talk between the two men. She would clean her new surroundings, wash clothes, prepare the following day's dinner. Depending on her mood, different songs would drift into her head – one after another stirring in her consciousness. There were children's chants, soothing lullabies, the frenzied rhythms of mouth music or "puirt a 'beul", laments and keening for the dead.

There came a time, however, when these last songs were the only ones that echoed.

Her son was killed; his brakes failing as he turned the corner of a hill. His lorry crashed through the wall of a bridge, coming to a halt in the water of the river below. They found him there with his neck broken, his heart soundless and still.

If the loss was hard for her to bear, it seemed even crueller on her father. She watched him dwindle from that day on. His breath, which even before had been sluggish and forced, now had to be coaxed to stir from his body. His meals would be pushed aside by his hand. There were nights when she would prise open his mouth with her fingers to ensure he had obtained a little food to eat.

Yet worst of all there were the voices.

She would hear them at all times of the day and night from the shadows of his bedroom. In the beginning, they seemed harmless. It was clear that the old man was experiencing once again the joys and troubles of his childhood. Quarrels with his old play-mates were being fought once again; former friendships renewed. As the previous generations found new life on his tongue, it became apparent that to his eyes past memories had turned into realities and the realities which had surrounded him for years blurred and faded into memories.

"Mammy," he slobbered like a child, "why can't I go out?"

His lungs begged him to stop speaking, sobbing between each word. For all that, he continued to talk. Sometimes his mouth would hiss in anger. He would suddenly recognise Murdag, his voice startling her as she worked around his bedside.

"You harlot!" he would cry. "You come back here in that condition, expecting us to care for your child!"

The words he had stifled all those years before tumbled out, barbed with a new and bitter hatred. She shivered when she heard him, recoiling from the fury of his voice as it rose in accusation, but no sooner was there silence for a moment than he would cry out again, his thin limbs thrashing the covers of his bed.

"We are the ones who will have to bear the burden of your disgrace! We are the ones who will suffer!"

She tried to get away from him, but she could hear his voice wherever she was in his home. It rumbled below her feet as she stood upstairs; whispered as she cooked his dinner in the kitchen. For weeks it seemed as if the entire house had turned against her; its every corner storing the memory of the day she had returned home expecting a stranger's child. Reminders of her disgrace threw shadows on the staircase, ruined the pride she had once taken in the kitchen her father had created with his tools.

It was at that time she locked the door of her home, refusing all help from her neighbours. She could hear them tap at her windows and doors, asking if she was all right, but she would close her eyes and ears and try to ignore them, shutting them out of her life. She didn't want them to know what her father was saying, afraid it might help them recall the events of some twenty odd years before when it seemed that every voice in the village had crowded into her thoughts. "She should be ashamed," they kept saying. "She should be ashamed..." She was afraid she might have to live through the humiliation of these days all over again.

And then one October morning she went into his room to find the blankets on his bed had hardly been disturbed. Her father lay still under the covers, only looking up when she had entered the room.

"Murdag."

She walked up to him tentatively, wondering if this peaceful greeting was only an illusion; a prelude to yet another round of spiteful accusations. But from the moment she looked at him she knew her old, lost father had returned. His eyes were full of a tired and painful kindness; his lips set in a sick and weary smile. Sitting down, she watched as his hand crawled across the covers towards her. Compassionately, she took it, enfolding it with her own.

"You like this house?" he muttered.

She nodded in reply.

"Promise me something then," he said.

"What?"

His lips mumbled dryly; the words dying, voiceless. She took a glass of water and set it to his mouth, watching the movement of his throat as he sipped the liquid down. Before he tried to speak again, he waved his arm around the sides of the bedroom; the panelled door, the fireplace, the window all brought under the flourish of his hand.

"Keep it as it is," he muttered. "No changes. Keep it the way it is exactly. No changes." He stared at her, his eyes wide and intense. Roused, it was almost as if he were daring her to defy him. "You promise me that?"

She nodded once again.

"That's good," he mumbled. "Good."

They were almost the last words he spoke. After this, his mouth could only foam as he attempted to talk, his hands beating against the blankets like a spoiled child in his frustration at being denied a voice. But still, she held onto him, waiting there until the last wheeze of his breath had silenced and she could find no trace of a pulse. It was only then she released him, closing the door of the house behind her as she went to a neighbour's home for the first time in months. She would ask there for help in preparing her father's corpse.

Flight

"We're leaving here, Iain," Mum said, her hand clutching a cotton hankie.

"What? Is Dad coming with us?" I asked.

She shook her head. "No. He's not coming."

"You're sure?"

"Yes. I'm sure." She rose to her feet and made her way to the bedroom. "We're going back to Grandad, you and I."

As I followed, I didn't know whether to believe her. I could only hope she was telling the truth. It would mean an end to all the fights I had seen between her and Dad. There had been lots of them, flaring up in a thousand different places: from a public park to a café; from a supermarket to the rooms of our flat. There was only one thing these occasions held in common. In each of them, Mum and Dad would use their Gaelic to hide the reasons for their arguments from me.

"No. Dad's not coming," Mum repeated, staring at the suitcase on the floor. "He's staying here while we're going to live with your Grandad, somewhere far away from Glasgow. There's no chance of him coming after us either. No money. He'd drink his last penny rather than spend it on a ticket home."

Mum raised her head again, trying to smile, and began to pull her clothes out of the wardrobe. Her camel coat was thrown on top of the suitcase, lying beside the blue dress flung over moments before. Watching her, I remembered some of the fights I had seen in this room, the way Dad's face turned as red as his hair as they screamed at each other. Listening to the strangeness of their words, I had become convinced that Dad was planning to send me away and Mum doing her best to keep me. I wanted to help Mum, join on her side, but the one time I asked her to teach me Gaelic, she smiled sadly in reply.

"I don't see why you should bother with it. We've no plans to go home and it's no good to man or beast down here."

My fears got worse after that. Dad's words became more threatening and Mum's voice a whisper compared to the loudness of his rage. At night, I often imagined her giving into him, allowing him to have things his way. I'd wake up screaming and Mum would have to wait beside me till I managed to sleep once again.

She had moved to the chest-of-drawers now, hurling most of its contents into her case, forcing the lid down till the locks snapped in place. While she did this, she never stopped talking, her words frantic on her lips.

"I've phoned for a taxi. It'll be coming soon. Keep an eye out the window for it, will you? That's a good boy... I wonder what your Dad will do when he comes home. It's good that he's gone to Kilmarnock to look for that job. Otherwise, we'd never have escaped... God! There's no room in this case..."

She was still talking as we sat in the taxi, staying silent only for the few minutes it took to dab on her lipstick. This was something she did every morning and sometimes Dad could be seen with its little red stains dotting his mouth and cheek. "It's like cutting yourself shaving," he would say, cleaning his face with a hankie. As her voice continued, I kept my attention on the meter. The way its numbers clicked and changed was a bit like seeing the countdown for a space-rocket on telly. Our trip felt something like that too, as if we were heading for a new planet to start our lives again.

"You'll meet your Grandad for the first time," she muttered. "He's a nice man. He's got a croft. Lots of sheep too. You'll enjoy running after them. I know I did at your age. And at least he doesn't drink. Not like your Daddy... That's one thing I won't be missing." She threw her arm around my shoulder, smiling grimly. "We'll be better off without him, won't we?"

I nodded my head, but already she had shifted to a new topic, comparing the open spaces of her island home with the walls and buildings of Glasgow. I hardly listened to her. To my mind, only one thing mattered. We were free of Dad now. Mum and I could be on our own...

We were on the plane when her voice finally came to a halt. She sat there stiffly, her fingernails white as they dug into the armrests. I was beside her, next to the window. As we took off, I saw the runway disappear, its tarmac giving way suddenly to green.

"This is great," I laughed as the plane rose. "Isn't it Mum?"

She nodded, her face chilled and white. She looked so sad so I leaned over and kissed her cheek.

"What's that for?" she asked.

"Oh... I'm just glad to be here."

"Yes," she sighed. "So am I. But be quiet just now. Your mum's tired... try not to bother her for a while."

My eyes returned to the window. It was a fine, hot day and the people on the ground looked tiny, like currants as they dotted the streets. I wondered if Dad was among them, small enough to be crushed by my finger. It was then I remembered he was looking for a job in a place called Kilmarnock. Mum gave a look of irritation as I asked her if we were passing it on our way.

"I'm not sure. Maybe."

I decided the town we were passing could only be Kilmarnock. It was filled with sandstone buildings that looked so small I felt sure I could smash them with the edge of my hand. Walking down one street, I could make out the dark outline of a man. He seemed to have thick ginger hair, the light blue suit Dad had worn that morning. I trapped him under my thumb, squashing down on his body. When I lifted my hand a few moments later, there was only my thumb print left on the glass. I rubbed this out, laughing as I turned to face Mum.

"It's all right, Mum," I informed her. "I've made sure Dad won't find us any more."

Mum's eyes were closed as she raised her finger to hush me. My gaze went back to the window. We were over the sea now, miles and miles of water with nothing in sight apart from a fishing boat or two. The distance made me feel safe. What Mum had said was right. There was no chance of Dad coming to chase after us.

An announcement crackled over the intercom. Its words made Mum prop herself up in the seat, pointing to the stretch of land we were approaching. Its rocks and moor took me by surprise, somehow managing to appear out of nowhere.

"That's the Isle of Harris," she declared.

"Does that mean we're nearly there?"

"Yes. It won't be long now."

My hands felt clammy. "That means we're not really that far from Glasgow?"

"Yes. I suppose it does," Mum laughed. "With the boats and planes they use these days, we're not half so far away as we used to be."

"We're not?"

"No. When I was a wee girl, we were an awful lot further." She smiled, handing me one of the barley sugars she held clenched in her hand. "Here. Take this, Iain. You'll need it in a moment or two."

Mum fastened my seat-belt as I unwrapped the sweet. I crunched it between my teeth as the plane began to go down. This time, it was my fingernails that turned white as I dug them into the chair's tartan arm-rests.

There was a bump, two or three more bumps and then the roll of tyres along the tarmac. My fingers gripped deeper as I willed the plane to stop. When it finally did so, the world looked much the same as ever, though it was flatter and greyer with its buildings a little smaller and shabbier than they had been in Glasgow. A few people were crowded near the doorway of one. Mum leaned over and waved frantically towards them, eager to gain somebody's attention.

"Your Grandad," she explained.

I screwed up my eyes to try and see where he was.

"There," she said, pointing out the window.

I looked again. The only man I could make out properly had thick red hair. I shivered as I thought of Dad.

"I can't see him," I said.

Mum bent over me to open my seat-belt. "Come on," she muttered impatiently. "You'll see him in a minute."

I left my seat reluctantly, following Mum down the passage. She was a few paces ahead of me, her shoulder-bag swinging on her arm. There was a blonde stewardess waiting at the exit, smiling politely at the passengers as they left. She looked smart in her tartan uniform as she reached out to shake Mum's hand.

"I hope you enjoyed your flight."

"Yes... Yes. We certainly did," Mum assured her.

Her fingers stretched in my direction, ruffling my hair. "I could see you did anyway," she grinned.

I moved away from her, stiffening with resentment. I didn't like anyone touching me like that. Slowly I climbed down the aeroplane steps. Mum was a foot or two ahead of me, as we made our way to the ground. I looked at the people in the doorway to see whom she was greeting, but there was no way I could tell. A lot of folk were waving their hands in welcome. As I came near them, I only wanted to turn round and head back to the plane.

A short, grey tubby man came towards Mum, rushing out of the crowd. He gathered her waist in his arms, his callused fingers on the back of her coat. He wore a dark-brown suit, a tight cloth cap that made a deep ridge in his forehead. His blue eyes were glittering and bottom lip shaking as he held her. Mum was sobbing too, her words muffled by his shoulder. Grandad reached out his hand to soothe her, running his fingers through her hair.

I looked up nervously, wondering what was going on.

Finally, Mum and Grandad broke away from each other. The old man looked down at me. The smudge of lipstick below one of his eyes wrinkled as he smiled.

"Agus an e seo Iain?" he said, turning to Mum.

I stood back when I heard this, feeling more frightened than ever. He had spoken in Gaelic. This meant an argument could start at any minute with unknown words being yelled across the tarmac, shouted by a pair of angry voices. I was just about to run back to the plane when Grandad's hands swept down, lifting me off my feet.

"Tha e cho breagha rium fhèin," he grinned.

He held me a few feet above the ground, his arms stretched at a distance. It was then I started kicking and screaming, aiming my feet at his waist and legs.

"No! No! Let me go! Don't take me with you! Let me go!"

He continued to hold me, though, his face furrowed with concern. Mum came to his side, placing her hand on my shoulder.

"What's wrong, Iain?" Grandad said in English. "Tell me what's the matter?"

It was Mum who answered. Moving forward, she began to stroke my hair with her hand. "I don't know," she muttered. "But he'll be all right soon, won't you, Iain? You'll be all right soon."

A Special Deliverance

The Reverend Malachy Fraser, minister of the parish of Cairnbost to his brother, Mr John Mitchell Fraser, headmaster, Helensburgh.

I beg pardon for the delay in writing this letter which I promised some time ago, but the Lord has given me an arduous and difficult task in the month since my arrival in this place – much more difficult than any I could have imagined before my coming.

I shall endeavour to explain what occurred here during the first weeks of my ministry. On a Monday evening during the last week of April a small boat – or sgoth – set out from the village of Cairnbost, accompanied by another from the neighbouring village of Bernisdale. It was a calm, clear night; the sea stiller than it has any right to be at that uncertain time of year. Yet the following evening – the weather as clement as it had been the day before – only one boat returned. The vessel from Cairnbost, together with the twelve men who had sailed on it, had completely disappeared.

Throughout that evening and the following morning, the search began. The men from Bernisdale were questioned over the whereabouts of their former companions. They informed us that the two boats had anchored alongside each other the previous evening, the crews spending the night sleeping and resting before shooting their fishing-lines at dawn. A few hours later, the two vessels had drifted apart from each other; the Cairnbost boat heading north. It was the last time the Bernisdale men caught sight of their friends and neighbours.

It is hard to imagine the grief these people displayed on hearing this news. They wept and wailed; they keened and beat their chests, imagining some freak wave had swept away their loved ones together with their boat. Yet this was not the conclusion of the tale, for an hour or so later, a message came from the villagers of Leagarry some five miles or so to our north. The Cairnbost boat had been found beached upon its sands – the vessel completely undamaged with its oars placed neatly across its thwarts. There was more even than this, however, to create perplexity among the populace. A few personal possessions – such as an oilskin-covered Bible; a roughly-woven tweed jacket; a grey brimmed hat which one of the crewmen, a young married man named Calum Macritchie, wore at all times on his head – were also to be found on board.

It was not my task to question what had happened to the crew of this vessel. Instead, it was my sad responsibility to bring this last item to his widow and inform her of her husband's disappearance. The wind had risen by then, blowing bitterly across our flat, unsheltered part of the island, but even its uproar was not enough to muffle the sound of her mourning. She clutched her young son – barely four months old – as she wept and howled, her cries preventing her from hearing the poor words of comfort I had to offer. As I sat there attempting to reason with her, I felt, not for the first time, my inadequacy at this type of task. It is a failing of mine that I am ill-at-ease in the company of women. God has not granted me the manner with which I might win their trust.

Yet from every trial, the Lord gives us strength. From every battle we lose, He grants us a small victory. Over the last few weeks, I have been given every opportunity to correct my former weakness. I have spent a great deal of my time attending these widows and their families, attempting to bring them the comforts of faith. For the most part, I have been successful; my only failure being Gormel Macritchie, the young widow whom I mentioned earlier in my letter. Half-maddened by grief, the deterioration in her appearance shows the state of her mind and spirit. A plump, olive-skinned girl with raven-coloured hair and a strong constitution, she no longer pays any attention to her appearance, leaving her locks uncombed and unplaited. Despite her evident hostility to my arrival at her home, I go there almost nightly to attend to the healing of her spirit and soul.

Fragment of slate, found in the ruins of the old manse, Cairnbost.

a for apil   a for appil   b for bol   c for cat   c for cat   d for dog   e for eg
e for eg   f for

Mr John Mitchell Fraser, headmaster, Helensburgh, to the Reverend Malachy Fraser, minister of the parish of Cairnbost, October 1850.

Though we were very pleased to see your recent visit to the family home, there is no doubt that we also felt great concern and alarm. There was, for instance, the state of your general health and appearance. It was clear – even from a glance – that the attack of gravel and stomach pains of which you complained earlier this year has much affected your physical well-being. The gauntness of your face and the shadows under your eyes could inform any observer of that sad fact. There is little doubt, too, that the conditions you suffered in your manse throughout the winter months have contributed a great deal to these problems. I find it hard to think of your home with its draughts and thick swirls of smoke without shivering with distaste. Surely the members of your church could help you with these things, even if they were only to provide you with a pathway across the stretch of bog and rush that leads to your door.

Yet our greatest concern has to be with the human isolation you clearly suffer. The Lord did not make man to be alone on this earth. He provided him with woman to be his helpmate and comfort. It is time for you to take the advice of St Paul and take a wife in order to end the loneliness of your situation. One realises that given your position, living on an island where there are few civilised or cultured women around, this would be no easy matter. It is for this reason that we do not suggest putting an end to your unmarried state in the usual, conventional manner. Instead, we would propose that either you leave the entire concern in the hands of your family or instead, advertise for a partner in the pages of a respectable Christian journal. With either course of action, it would not be long before a suitable choice of partner would be found.

Fragment of paper.

he is a good man hoo can looc after yung torcil and myself in his mans even if i doo not caer for him the wai a woman is sipoest to caer for hur husband still mabye i shood taec him wot els doo i haf too looc forwart to

The Reverend Malachy Fraser to his brother, Mr John Mitchell Fraser, May 1851.

As I write these words today, I tremble – and not for the usual reasons as the men from the village have finally helped to end the draughts that have made me shake with ague and fever throughout my time here. Instead, I shake with awe and wonder at the Lord and His kindness. He has provided me with a partner to put an end to the loneliness and isolation I have suffered throughout the last years.

Her name is one I have mentioned in my letters before – Gormel Macritchie, the young widow whose husband disappeared when the fishermen of Cairnbost were spirited away in such strange circumstances a number of years ago. I may also have mentioned how in the early days of her grief, she reacted to my appearance with all too evident hostility and dislike, but as time went on, her initial reaction changed. Her heart softened and she accepted first Christ and then – wooed by my fumbling attempts to teach her to read and write – my unworthy self. In these circumstances, it was only natural that when like a number of others whose men were lost at sea, she felt it was time to begin her life again, she should turn to me for support and affection.

Even at this very moment, I can almost hear my mother declaring that the choice of a Hebridean fisherman's widow is not a suitable match for a man in my position. However, if they met, I feel quite certain she would change her mind. She would see then what a fine person she is – the depth of her affections evident in the way in which she mourned for her former husband. She is also a woman of both intelligence and strength, possessing the kind of strong, muscular frame that is necessary for survival in this part of the world. Finally – and this is most important of all – she is a woman of faith; one who has embraced the Saviour fully in her life. Persuade my mother of these matters, dear brother, and you gain not only my gratitude, but also, I am certain, both the gratitude and prayers of the faithful among my flock.

Fragment of paper.

i often sai these things in my hed, but toodai i rite them down on paper sure i will go mad if i dont find someone to say thees things too he is not my husband yet he has not joint wit me as a bool joins wit a cow or a stalyon wit a mair or as mi poor ded husban calum did wit me oll those yeers ago it is not that he dus not tri but he fails his bod as smoll and soft as a cutaig

The Reverend Malachy Fraser to Dr Gordon MacBain, medical practitioner in the town of Maransay, April 1856 – unsent and uncompleted.

I am writing to you on a difficult and sensitive matter where I trust I can rely on your complete discretion and assistance.

My problem lies in the marriage bed where I have been unable to

Mr John Mitchell Fraser, Helensburgh, to Reverend Malachy Fraser, August 1857.

News has reached my ears this morning which was of clearly such great import to you and your personal happiness that I hastened to lift up my pen and paper, writing out this letter which you now hold in your hands.

Knowing I had family connections with the Outer Hebrides, a ship's captain from the Orkneys called Anderson sought me out. He told me he had been in the West Indies and come across a trading ship while at anchor there. He had met several of the crew, including a young Gaelic-speaking islander who had told him, with some hesitancy and difficulty, that together with a number of his fellow-crewmen, he had been press-ganged while fishing in the waters around his native island. Thinking of me, Captain Anderson had questioned him further, asking him what part of the islands he came from. The boy had replied – and in this either the ship-captain's memory or the boy's English is at fault – "Carnabos".

So there it is, my young brother, a tale to make of what you will. I thought, however, that this piece of information should be passed onto you as a matter of urgency as clearly it may have a great effect on your future life.

Fragment of paper.

Sumthin is the matter wit the minister he spends his nites wocing the flore and prayin he tocs to himself lifting up the bible and loocing throo its pajes serchin for sum help that he cannot find nuthin seems to help him the onli time i poot my arms around him he maed too hit me agen

Reverend Malachy Fraser to Mr John Mitchell Fraser, September 1857.

I have often confessed to you my lack of ease with women, how I have no understanding of them or their ways. Once again I have been shown proof of this – my failure to comprehend them abundantly clear even in my dealings with the woman I chose to share my home.

It all came about when I decided to tell Gormel about the content of your letter. I took a great deal of time and patience over this, explaining to her how there was even doubt over whether her husband had actually been on board the ship the captain had discovered; that, even if he had been, the vessel had been docked in the West Indies, a great distance away, and was unlikely ever to come home; that, given his situation, it was likely that her former husband had – like her – started a new life for himself.

She remained unconvinced by all my fine words and assurances. Within moments, her whole personality was transformed. Instead of being rational about the situation, she babbled on about her fisherman had been her true and natural husband, being the only man with whom she had a child. She even went so far as to cast aspersions on my manhood, making a few foul and unfeminine remarks too crude to be repeated here.

Events were to surprise me still further. She went on her knees, embracing young Torquil and telling him that his father was still alive. She also told me that she planned to go to the town of Maransay and wait for him at the harbour there. During the time she was away, he was instructed to go and live at his grandmother's home. As the two of us have never got on – the boy being too insolent and disrespectful for my liking – he readily agreed to this suggestion.

Within an hour or so, she was away. She sojourned down the road to Maransay, her few belongings in a bag draped over her shoulder. When I spoke to her sister's husband, hoping that he would attempt to restrain her, he dismissed my words, claiming I was not man enough to keep her. As a consequence, I was reduced to watching her disappear into the distance.

I cannot say I have not been at fault in this situation. I never obtained the degree of submissiveness a man has a right to expect from a wife. She was too strong-willed for me, employing all the stratagems and devices her sex is prone to use in order to obtain her own way. It is that very will that endangers her now. She is quite deluded and disturbed at present, bent on a course of action that is destined to end in madness and despair.

I would be grateful for your prayers and any advice you can give me on how to proceed further in this situation. I have taken it upon myself to write to the Baron Baillie, informing him of my predicament and asking for his assistance.

Reverend Malachy Fraser to Mr Evander Matheson, The Baron Baillie, Maransay, September 1857.

I write to inform you, sir, of the probable arrival in your town of my wife, Gormel Fraser or Macritchie. She left home yesterday in the expectation of finding her former husband, Calum Macritchie, a young fisherman who disappeared from the district in strange circumstances a number of years ago.

If she appears in the harbour area of the town, I would be grateful if the young woman could be taken into protective custody. She is in a state of hysteria at present, believing her first husband to be alive. As a result, she has deserted the family home and I fear that there will be greater consequences still, once the inevitable happens and she is doomed to disappointment. She may yet seek to put an end to her own life.

In order to assist you in this task, I wish to provide you with a physical description of my wife. She has a sturdy constitution, bordering on plumpness, long black hair, olive-shaded skin and blue eyes. She wears the long brown dress and coarse tweed jacket customarily worn by the country woman of the island.

If you find her, I would be grateful if you could attempt to reason with her. It is a task quite beyond me at present – my charity and patience quite exhausted – but I appeal to you as a devout and faithful fellow-Christian for your help.

Notice written with charred stick and nailed to wall of harbour building.

calum macreechie fisherman cairnbost i wait for you now forever and olwais

Mr Evander Matheson, Baron Baillie, Maransay, to the Reverend Malachy Fraser, minister, Cairnbost.

Your letter arrived with me three days ago and since then I have tried my utmost to deal with the situation presented in its pages.

The physical description you provided of your wife was almost unnecessary. Strangers are rare enough in this place for any to be noticed within moments of their arrival, and your wife – let us say – has been more distinctive than most. The citizens of Maransay have been all too aware of her presence among us over the last few days. She has spent some of her time questioning the town's sailors and fishermen over the whereabouts of her former husband, occasionally showing them a grey, brimmed hat she clutches tightly in her hand. During the remainder of her time, she has either been sheltering in the doorway of one of the harbour offices looking outwards to the mouth of the harbour or making her way to the lighthouse that stands on the headland, leaning against its wall. It is as if she expects to see her former husband appear at any moment – a Neptune standing upright among the waves of the sea.

There is only one thing that seems to shake her constancy – the approach of any man in her direction. She flees then, lifting her skirts around her knees and running. There was one time when that physical strength you mentioned in your letter was apparent. She knocked down a man who tried to grab her, escaping easily from his grasp. It was this response that made it hard for us to place her in custody, but eventually, we succeeded, bringing her to my office.

Within the room, it was possible to look at her more closely. Her physical condition was badly dishevelled with her clothes filthy and torn and her hair matted with dirt and tears. It was also clear that her body was covered with an array of cuts and bruises. Her eye and mouth was swollen. Scratches could be seen on her legs and arms.

She displayed some of these wounds in response to my questions about her tale – one which I found incredible and will be repeated only in these pages here. She claimed that you continually beat and misused her, treating her not with the warmth due to a wife but with the coldness and cruelty one might display to a slave. She then went on to give an account of the more intimate aspects of your married life which any woman of modesty – or even a vestige of sanity – would have withheld from a male audience.

It seems to me imperative that she is not given any opportunity to repeat these tales to any further audience as it clearly would do much damage to your standing in this or any other community. There is no doubt, for instance, that her scars and wounds would give much credence to her story, especially in the eyes of common folk who are only too inclined to believe the very worst of their betters.

It is in view of this that I have been forced to reach certain conclusions. I would consider it desirable for you to leave the parish of Cairnbost as soon as practical and for some other minister to take over your charge. If this story ever became common property, it would cause nothing but scandal, damaging the standing and good work of all ministers of the gospel on the island. For the sake of the future of Christ's message in this place, it is essential that this does not happen.

It is also necessary that your wife be placed in a place of detention for the insane on the mainland as soon as it can possibly be arranged.

Reverend Malachy Fraser to Mr Evander Matheson, The Baron Baillie, Maransay, October 1857.

I am forced to agree with the course of action suggested in your recent letter. I will be leaving this parish as soon as a replacement can be organised.

Fragment of paper.

i am waiting for you calum i will wait for you forever.

Gorbachev in Stornoway

How can I, that girl standing there,
My attention fix
On Roman or on Russian
Or on Spanish politics?...
Politics – W B Yeats

(An extract from the memoirs of Dmitri Gerenko, Special Adviser to Mikhail Gorbachev, former President of the Soviet Union.)

It was Raisa who began our problems that day. Only a few hours before our departure, she made her intentions clear, her high heels sparking as she strutted through the corridors of the Kremlin.

"I will go to Reykjavik," she declared.

The President sighed as he always did when his wife was at her most determined. "Try and dissuade her, Dmitri," he said to me. "Mrs Reagan will not be there. It will not be good diplomacy if she comes along."

I scurried in Raisa's wake as I tried to make her husband's position plain: that this was an important summit meeting, not a PR exercise for the Western media; that Nancy was an important influence on her husband and would not take kindly to her presence; that her very arrival on the plane would be a signal to General Bolgarov and his anti-Western camp that the President was too much under his wife's control to be a man with whom they could do business. But a single haughty look from Raisa was enough to silence all my protests. A couple of hours later and she would be on that plane, her bags packed with the furs and dresses he – privately – deplored, setting off on another expedition to the shops and stores of the decadent West.

And so it turned out to be. Raisa sat behind us as we travelled on the plane that day – the men in the party discussing what weapons we should hoard or surrender in the SALT talks with Reagan over the next few days.

"Do not give too much away," General Bolgarov kept saying, his dark eyebrows as ominous as thunderclouds. "Let us keep as much as we can."

"We need to make some strides towards a lasting peace, Comrade General," Gorbachov explained. "Otherwise our economy..."

It was in the midst of this conversation that the plane began shuddering – its engines trembling as we travelled over the coastline of Norway. Its fjords and cliffs stretched out like fingers threatening to clutch us from our position in the skies.

"There is a fault in our electrics," the pilot declared. "We will do our best to repair it while we are in flight, but we may have to land."

Raisa gibbered in alarm at his words, no doubt foreseeing a moment when the sealskin hat that decorated her head might be restored to its former owners.

"I should have stayed at home," she mumbled in panic. "Mikhail! Why did you ask me to come with you? I should never have listened to you."

Again, that sigh and look of exasperation on the President's face. For a moment, I found myself thinking of all the unhappiness of his domestic life; how he had told me so many times of his longing for the simple peasant women who had cared for him in his childhood, ones without any thought for the furs and perfumes that Raisa garnished round her life. "A plain honest-to-goodness woman," he told me one time after he had slipped down a few glasses of vodka. "That's who a man like me would love to meet. But what chance does a man in my position have to do so? So many faces in a crowd. So many seeking power. And in every embrace – even those of my relatives – there may be the kiss of a Judas."

Yet an instant later, the President expelled this unsought pity from my head. He had been listening to the noise of the engine and come to a decision.

"Get the pilot to find an airport we can land. Nothing must endanger what we are about to do."

I nodded in obedience. Listening to his clipped commands, all thought of Gorbachev the private man vanished and my sense of him as our country's leader was restored.

And that was how we arrived in Stornoway – the plane curling round to land on a flat, treeless island on the north-western edge of Britain. We went down the steps to find our only welcome was a brisk wind that braced and blew. As I drew up my collar to protect my face from its attentions, a memory of my childhood in Tarivostok – a small town in the north-eastern part of Siberia – came to my mind.

An airport worker dressed in red overalls gaped as a party of Soviet generals and heavy-set men in thick coats and Astrakhan hats marched towards him down the runway. His eyes widened even more as he recognised the President and his wife.

"Where can we wait?" General Bolgarov barked out his question, his military manner never deserting him even in these strange circumstances.

The man pointed towards a little grey building which lay at the edge of the tarmac, dwarfed by the large RAF hangers around it.

"Thank you," he pronounced, leading our delegation through its back door. On one side, there was what probably passed for the Baggage Retrieval Area – a row of steel rollers built at a slant for luggage to roll down. On the other, there was a doorway leading to a small room where coffee and tea could be served. We barged in there, disturbing the terminal's only customers – a number of unshaven men nursing their cold cups of coffee and playing cards.

One of them was just placing a trio of Aces on the table when we entered, muttering something in his astonishment that was clearly not English.

"Co bho ghrian...? A Mhafia?"

It was then that Raisa entered. She bustled in behind us, accompanied by her secretary – a thin, leaf-like figure with brown hair and a lime-green suit – and all the time, she was snapping questions, directing them at everyone in her party.

"General Bolgarov... where did you say we were? Oh, and how long did you say we'd be here? Is there anywhere we can go while we're waiting? Mikhail, do you think there are any reasonable shops in this place?"

Even that famous red birthmark seemed to grow pale as he sat down, listening to the words of his wife.

"No," he said. "I don't think this is either the time or the place."

Raisa's brown eyes flashed. "Very well, Comrade President," she declared as she glided over in the card-players' direction. "We will do as you say." A moment or two later, however, we heard the words "Woolworths" and "Harris Tweed" emerging from their conversation. The card-players' eyes sparkled as they imagined tips much larger than the sums that ever could be won at an airport poker game.

It was then something happened which I believe changed the whole course of history. A waitress arrived at our table. She had long, black hair, brown eyes and sallow skin – looking for all the world like a senorita washed up on this cold, northern shore – and a tall, full-breasted form which her shabby red waitress outfit rounded and emphasised. Some thirty years of age, she moved quietly between the tables, placing cups of tea and coffee before the military men and Communist Party officials who were her unexpected guests.

Something happened to the President when he saw her. His breath piped down to a whistle. His fingers drummed a tattoo onto the cafe table.

"Look at her," he muttered. "Look at her."

"Yes, Comrade President."

"Her uniform has a hole at the elbow. There is a run in her tights. Can you imagine how Raisa would behave if she was dressed like that?"

My eyes scuttled in the direction of our country's First Lady, wrapped in a swathe of furs and asking for directions to the town's shops. "No, Comrade President."

As she headed in our direction, other aspects of her appearance became clearer. The cuffs of her white sweater were dirty and frayed. Her black skirt was worn and thin. And at the sight of all this – a man who had never blanched before the sparkle of a tiara or the power of a general's insignia – there was a tremor in his voice.

"Coffee or tea?" she asked.

"I... I... I'll h... h... have coffee," he answered, his translator by his side.

The waitress nodded, noting his order on her pad, and moved back to her tiny kitchen at the side of the terminal. The President's eyes haunted her footsteps as she walked across the room, noting her every step and sway; the grace with which she wore her shabby uniform.

And then he seemed to rouse himself from his distraction. He shook his head at his own bemusement and turned to me with a dark and earnest look on his face.

"You know what I would like most in the world, Dmitri? To have a woman like that for my own." He lifted his eyes once again to watch her pouring water from a kettle. "But the world does not permit me such simplicities. Perhaps it will one day."

History records most of what happened after that.

The meeting in that other Icelandic "White House" where Reagan and the President bargained half the world's weapons away. Where men like General Bolgarov and the executives of defence industries watched and raged in disbelief. Where ordinary people felt for the first time this century that peace might be possible. Where the world media snapped pictures of Raisa as she hurried through Reykjavik's shops and schools, gaining more acclaim and belongings.

Yet there is more to tell than that. There was the morning some months after his replacement by President Yeltsin that Mikhail returned to Stornoway airport. A frail and haunted figure, he dodged through the crowd

70

that had gathered there. A number wore dark suits and Homburg hats; many with stiff white halos that had slipped around their corpulent necks. They were circling around a rather straight-laced young woman who appeared to be wearing a shapeless stretch of sackcloth rather than a dress.

"Yes. He did touch me," she was saying. "I swear he did."

Her words were greeted by a squeal of triumph by one of the men who had assembled there. "We've got him now," he declared. "We've got him now!"

Watching their behaviour, Gorbachev momentarily regretted ever having liberated religion in the Soviet Union, yet he was even more appalled by how much the terminal had changed. A bar was in place where the waitress had once poured her kettle; her replacement a young woman just out of her teens with a tiny metal stud fixed in her right nostril and dark mascara smeared around her eyes. Nevertheless, he went up to her, clutching a piece of paper on which he had written some phrases he had long since learned by heart.

"Where is she? Where is she? Where is the black-haired woman who work here?"

The girl briefly halted her relentless chewing of spearmint to answer his question. "Sorry. Ah dinnae ken whit yer oan aboot."

Baffled, he walked away from her, blending into the group of men wearing similar clothes to those he had on that day. Too busy talking to the woman they had been speaking to earlier, they didn't even appear to notice him when he joined their flight off the island. They were going to their annual Assembly, while he was heading back to Moscow to begin his life again.

The Clearances

How David had come to be there he did not know, but for the first time he realised there was something new and different about his surroundings that morning.

He became aware of this as he walked down to the foreshore. Standing among the large, grey rocks and withered heather, there were the remains of a number of old and roofless houses. Green moss and lichen coated their walls and, sheltered by the stones, a field of nettles and thistles stirred back and forth, their tall, jagged stalks shifting in the wind. For a few moments he stood there, examining the earth, the darkness of the sea nearby, and wondered what kind of men had ever lived in this place. It could have been a bunch of bearded weirdos, desperate to keep away from the world.

Breath misty in the air, he climbed the hill beyond the ruins. There was an old, grey-haired man working on its crest, a cloth bonnet tight upon his head. He was digging a drain to allow water to escape from a bog that had just formed there. There was the squelch and crunch of soil as he shoved the blade down. The water oozed, trickling down the slope. David watched it rush before it disappeared into the ground.

It was only then the man noticed him. Face reddened by wind and work, he looked up. For a while, he seemed startled by David's appearance, staring at him before he spoke. "Hello," he said. Then there was a long pause. "I never saw you coming."

David found it equally hard to speak. It was as if he were recovering his voice after a long silence. "I wonder if you can help me," he muttered.

"I'll be glad to do that if I can," the old man answered.

"These old houses there – who lived in them?" he asked.

"Them?" The man flourished a hand in their direction. "They call the place Leagarry. A few families used to live there many years ago – until they were evicted by the landlord."

"Evicted?"

"Yes. It happened in the old days of the Clearances." He halted for a moment, noting the look of mystification on David's face. "But I forgot. You're one of those people from the new State houses. You're not from round here." His eyes gleamed with curiosity. "Where are you from anyway?"

For a moment, David couldn't remember, but suddenly the answer hurried to his lips. "Liverpool."

"You're from a lot of funny places, you crowd. Liverpool, Glasgow, Birmingham. There's even a West Indian family from Bristol. And we're not the only village on the island with new settlers. Most of the others have new folk too." The old man shook his head in wonder. "How are you enjoying it?"

"It's okay," David shrugged.

"I suppose it'll take a bit of getting used to, but it'll work out in the end. Especially with the cash they're offering with this Regional Transfer Scheme. It'll make a big difference to your family."

David nodded sullenly. Though he knew nothing about this, he decided he had to make some sort of response. In the distance, he could see the Instructors coming, their brown uniforms almost blending with the moor. These were the people who spent most of the day with his parents and brother, telling them how to weave, fish, cut peats for fuel. It was this last activity which had foxed his father completely. He had come home one evening with large, black patterns stretched across his back, his thumb red and gashed by the peat-iron blade.

"Tell me about the Clearances," David asked.

The old man smiled, telling him of the nearby villages that had been emptied to make farms, of the other places on the mainland where the same processes had been repeated, stories of Sutherland and Strathnaver, of how Patrick Sellar had burnt the roof of a house that an old woman had refused to leave…

They were talking about that when the Instructors arrived for David, taking him home.

He spent most of the rest of the day watching television. On an afternoon current affairs programme two politicians were on the screen – one from the Conservative government and the other from His Majesty's opposition – and they were talking about the problems of Britain's inner cities. They discussed the rioting which, one said, had "left no housing estate or run-down area in our urban landscape untouched", and the failure of the police and the major political parties to find a solution to this problem. "Something radical must be done," the older of the two statesmen said, briefly adopting a surgeon's vocabulary. "The problem must not be allowed to continue being a cancer in our society. It must be cut out and removed."

The other politician agreed, reminding him, however, that not all the inhabitants of our inner cities were rebelling against law and order. "Just a few are running sores on our society," he smiled reassuringly, "but there is one issue this country has to face. Isolated though these disruptive individuals are, they are symptomatic of a wider decay. It is clear that cities like Birmingham, Liverpool, Glasgow and Manchester, the great industrial cities of our past, no longer have a role in the economy of this country. They are historical anachronisms, relics of the Industrial Revolution. We should take steps to increase and develop Government projects like the Regional Transfer Scheme, to facilitate the removal of the inhabitants of our inner cities..."

As he struggled to make sense of all the politicians had said, David began to remember.

He began to remember the fighting that had occurred in the street below his bedroom window, the flare of the fire-bombs, the whine and smack of the plastic bullets. The police were armed with shields, rifles, and water-cannons; their opponents with petrol bombs, knives and guns. His older brother, Gary, was out there with the rioters. After five years of unemployment, the fighting had given him a new vigour, a new hope and strength in his life. It all seemed an age away from his existence now on the island.

Feeling giddy as he recalled this, David left his new home. It was a much better house than the one they had lived in before – its doors and windows freshly painted; floors newly carpeted; a large garden lying behind it, flourishing with the wide variety of vegetables the Instructors living next door had taught them how to plant – yet for all that, David was glad to escape, heading for the grey and crumbling ruin the old man had told him about.

When he reached there, he tried to imagine his old house looking like Leagarry; green lichen crusting its red brick, thistle and nettle carpeting its floor. He could remember what it looked like now. It had been a small apartment on the top floor of a two-storey building. The hum of the nearby motorway could always be heard within its walls, interrupted only by the sounds of a leaking tap the Council plumber had been unable to fix. With the paint that flaked from its doors and windows, the mould flowering on its walls, it didn't take too much effort to picture it in the same condition as Leagarry, wind and rain lolling open its doors.

As he sat there smoking one of the cigarettes the Instructors tried hard to

74

discourage, David began to remember what had happened the night they had left the city. The first thing that morning, the roadworks had been set up at either end of the street; pneumatic drills powering through the thin covering of tarmac, grey mounds of sludge and mud blocking the road entrances. When people had complained, their tongues were silenced by talk of two war-time bombs embedded in the road. "Sorry you can't do your shopping, missus, but would you prefer to be blown up?"

After darkness had fallen, the tanks and lorries arrived, the sound of their heavy wheels rumbling through the walls of the houses. It was then the police swarmed the estate. Their rifles at their ready, they had charged into the flats. David's mother had locked the door when she saw them, but a few kicks from a policeman's boot sorted that, and splinters of wood had spun in the air. Standing in the doorway, he had ushered them out with his gun.

"Come on, you lot! Down to the station!"

There were hundreds of folk in the Conningsby nick that day, all from the same small neighbourhood. David recognised faces in his own or neighbouring cells, people he had met before in street or school. Some sat disconsolately, while others – his brother, Gary, included – rattled the bars and cursed their jailers, telling them what would happen once they were released. The policemen smiled good-humouredly at their threats, escorting them to the Interrogation Room when their names were called.

It was towards evening when David's family were named. They were led into the Interrogation Room; Gary tussling with policemen as they dragged him there. Inside its door, they had been separated – each one taken to an individual cubicle. A young female doctor was scribbling at her desk when he entered, her desk-lamp giving her face a strange, shadowy quality; a sheen coming off her long, black hair. A policeman stood guard in the corner of the room.

"You're David Blackley?" she asked.

Dumbly, he nodded.

"Lie down on the table." She pointed to the board that stretched lengthways along the wall.

He did as she asked, watching her white coat and deft fingers as she unbuttoned his sleeve, rolling his shirt back to the elbow. He felt vaguely pleased as she did this. The woman had a clean, fresh look he had rarely seen among the women he knew. He liked the scent of her perfume.

"This might hurt a little," she said.

The woman patted David's shoulder reassuringly as she raised the hypodermic to the light…

After that, his memory fumbled. He could see the woman's face swirling, becoming distended and grotesque. The sound of her voice continued, turning flat and heavy until it merged with the silence that was crushing all his thoughts. From that moment, everything he saw seemed to swim behind a sheet of heavy glass. There was the vague recollection of being taken on board a plane, his senses dulled and slow. He remembered, too, the sombre voices of the Instructors telling him how the cities lacked a future, that it was the small towns and outlying regions that pointed the way to the world of tomorrow.

It was only this morning there had been a rebirth, a rediscovery of his own mind. It had happened when he came across the old, ruined homes of Leagarry, met the old man who had told him about the Clearances way back in Scotland's past. He felt sorry for these people, driven from their homes by landlord and soldier, their roofs sometimes burnt from above their heads by cruel, greedy men like Sellar. Thinking of this, David stubbed his cigarette, crushing its tip on the grey, stone wall. As he did this, a tiny red ember fell to the ground, steaming till he stamped on its glow with his foot. With the suddenness of his movement, the matchbox rattled in his pocket. He wrapped it in his handkerchief, trying to deaden the sound. It wouldn't do to let the Instructors know he was still pinching his father's cigarettes. It was a petty act of rebellion, he knew that – but it meant a lot to him – a sign that somewhere deep within, something of himself remained.

No – what Sellars had been part of, the old Clearances, should never have been done – and yet it seemed better than what was happening now. At least the people of that time had been left with their minds and memories. There had been no harsh, unrelenting Clearance of their thoughts.

He started to walk up the hill to the Instructors' House – this other people's history in his head, his hand clutching the box of matches through his handkerchief.

Season and Serve

Neck spilling from his dog-collar, Stewart's face smiled from the front page of the *Chronicle*. Trembling, Cathy put the newspaper down, heading for the kitchen table where there was a battered recipe book she had set aside the night before. In its pages were a list of the ingredients for the lentil and bacon broth she had been planning to make for ages.

1 oz (25 g) lard
8 oz (225 g) lentils, soaked and drained
3 oz (75 g) smoked bacon, chopped

She poured water from the bowl where lentils had been steeped, still shaking at the thought Colin might discover all that happened those years before. He wasn't the forgiving type. That was sure. His face – which had rounded and softened over the last few years – would grow hard and sharp again.

"What the hell were you playing at?"

Cathy would shrug to show she had no excuses, knowing at the same time this wasn't true. Colin had been a lorry driver back then, Cal Mac's crews seeing more of him than she did as they ferried him to and from the mainland roads. While he was at home, he still didn't behave like a member of the family, muttering and sighing when Moira and Peter made their eternal wails and demands.

"Can't you do something...?" he'd complain, his eyes skirting over the rows of clothes drying near the stove, the clutter of toys on the floor.

She wouldn't have the chance to answer before something else happened: Peter's plate skidding from his high chair; Moira emptying a bag-full of potatoes on the floor. He'd turn away from the kitchen with disgust paining his face, heading to the pub a few hours later to escape the disorder of home.

He wasn't like that nowadays. Instead, he would sit for hours watching television; the youngest boy, Allan, sitting in the crook of his arm. She would hear their words as she worked in the kitchen. They would have mock battles about some football match as she prepared their Sunday lunch – *"You were lucky there, boy..." "What do you mean by that, Dad? We were all over them..."* – or else they might sit in silent awe at the nature programmes

77

they both loved while she cut away at the pile of vegetables on the table.

8 oz (225 g) onions, chopped
8 oz (225 g) carrots, sliced
6 oz (175 g) celery, chopped

As her blade nicked neatly, she recalled how Stewart had interrupted her while she worked at a task like this. She had been preparing a Norwegian Apple Cake, the children asleep and ingredients stacked in front of her when he entered the kitchen.

4 large Bramley apples, peeled and sliced
2 large eggs
9 oz (250 g) sugar...

"You're busy," he said.

He had come in without her noticing; something that was easy to do with the back door always open. She smiled, taking in at a glance his small wiry frame; well-pressed, dark suit; thin, anxious face, blue-eyed and fresh, and the startling shock of his grey hair, at odds with so much of the rest of his appearance.

"Hello..."

"My name's Stewart MacIntyre. Your new insurance agent. Pleased to meet you."

He stretched out a hand to greet her, but she refused, the layer of flour on her fingers flourished by way of excuse.

"Oh, that's okay. You don't mind if I sit down at the table? I have to put this ledger somewhere. Weighs a ton..."

She gave him a cup of tea, some biscuits and a piece of her Almond Feather Cake, watching the delicacy with which he ate. He had huge hands – surprising and incongruous on his slender, small-boned frame – but he ate with a gentility and care that was almost effeminate, so unlike Colin's untidy way of eating. And there was, too, his easy banter, his relaxed and disarming grin.

He liked the Linda Ronstadt cassette she had playing in the kitchen, though he preferred Emmylou Harris' voice. *"I've always got her on in the car..."* He agreed with her about religion – *"Most of them are hypocrites."* – even though his father, dead for some years, had been a church elder. *"No."* He didn't have a girlfriend at the moment. *"Young enough. For all my grey hair, I'm still only twenty-six."* She nodded and said she thought like that now. She had gone out and got married *"far too young".*

Afterwards, he had told her that he felt drawn to her right away. It was

78

partly her baking. Her cake had melted between his teeth, making him come alive in the middle of a dull, tired day when he had spoken of little else but premiums. Each bite had sung in his throat; each chew and swallow almost as good as sex in restoring him. But there was, too, the look on her face. The fringe of her long, black hair tipped back by her fingers, he could see the shadows that darkened her eyes for a moment before they gave way to a smile. It gave her an aura of sadness which made him long to give her his strength and protection.

Their voices must have wakened Moira. Her tiny feet padded down the hallway to the kitchen door. Standing there, her hair framed her face like soft, brown corkscrews as she stared uncertainly into the room.

"And who's this little princess?" he grinned.

And almost magically, she approached him, her arms reaching out to be gathered in his lap.

> *1½ pints of chicken stock*
> *pinch of nutmeg*
> *salt and pepper*

"A cup of tea would be grand!" Colin's voice had yelled when she was in the kitchen.

She had brought it to his chair, her only thanks a nod as he stared at some American Football match on Sky. Allan sat opposite him, occasionally speaking when Colin asked him to explain some feature of the game. When he did this, the words rushed and stumbled from his mouth. Full of nervous energy, he was unable to sit still watching any match. His feet would kick imaginary footballs; dive in imitation of a rugby try. The older man would enjoy all this activity, grinning at the boy's restlessness. His other children had the same sturdy stillness he saw in himself, and he gained pleasure from the fact that Allan was different.

And then there was the way, too, that he had actually seen the boy grow up. During the ten years of Allan's life, he had worked on the island, driving a lorry for one of its building firms. Cathy preferred that. The word "married" had no meaning for people when there was no one facing them across the kitchen table or filling the other side of the bed.

Or so it had proved for her. She recalled the first day she had forgotten the wedding ring on her finger. Stewart's fingers had touched her back as she bent over to put some tea and cake on the table. (Victoria Sandwich. Astonishing how she remembered such details.) Moments later, his fingers were moving over the rest of her body, until she could feel the weight of his ribs on her chest, the arcing of his back, the meshing of bone and skin and body. When they had finished making love, he reached out to touch her side. "This is now bone of my bones, and flesh of my flesh," he said. "She shall be called Woman because she was taken out of Man."

His shoulders shook, his large hands clutching her so tightly that she could almost feel her bones crunch and the haze of his sweat fill the air around them. When she finally managed to turn round to look at him, she could see that his face was pale, his eyes red as he tried to blink back his tears.

"God, I love you," he whispered. "God, I love you."

And she, believing that he was talking to her, reached out once again towards him, taking him in...

Her fingers shook as she recalled this, nearly spilling the

half teaspoon of dried thyme

she was adding. When she had done this, she poured the rest of the mixture into the bacon and vegetables she had been frying over the last while. She spent the next few minutes wiping the kitchen surfaces while she waited for the pan to boil.

She had been waiting, too, for ages the last time he came to her home.

He had been avoiding her for a number of weeks; his red Ford Sierra rushing past in a drive to collect new policies, bonuses, or – she feared in her worst moments – conquests. In her kitchen cabinets, her freshly-baked Banana Cake and Lemon Sponge lay untouched, waiting for the day he would return to her. Yet now he was with her, he wouldn't touch a slice. His face was almost as grey as his hair as he spoke. Finally, he managed to prise out what he had come there to say.

"I've changed. You see, I've become a Christian."

He told her how it had happened. The cassette player in the car had been broken; the voices of Waylon Jennings, Willie Nelson, Tammy Wynnette silenced for a time. Switching radio stations, he had stumbled on a short, religious talk. A polite, Lowland accent had echoed in his car.

"If you've any troubles or you're concerned that your life has taken the wrong fork, a mistaken direction, take it to the Lord in prayer. He's there..."

"Take it to the Lord in prayer". It was an expression his father had used. *"You got troubles? Take it to the Lord in prayer..."* The words echoed from his childhood, startling him so much it was as if his father was speaking. He shook himself from his thoughts to see a young girl playing near a group of council houses running out in the middle of the road. The brakes squealed as he slammed them, stopping a few inches from where she was standing.

"All at once as I sat there, shaking behind that wheel, I started thinking about the way I was living. Stuck in a job I hated. Drinking too much. Carrying on... well, you know. And I could see how empty my existence was. What my father would have thought. What..."

He left his words unfinished, turning away and rubbing his eyes. She might have felt sorry for him if she hadn't troubles of her own. She hadn't had a period for the last two months. She felt sure she was carrying his child. But before she had time to tell him these things, he was heading out the door, babbling something as he retreated to the safety of his red Ford Sierra.

"I'm sorry, Cathy... I know it's awful for you, but I just can't carry on like this... I can't. My nerves couldn't stand it. I couldn't..."

She stood at the roadside, hearing the music of "Will The Circle Be Unbroken" echoing from the cassette player as he drove along. On the back seat, she noticed a black-covered Bible half-hidden by a pile of insurance brochures. And her own face, too, reflected in the window. Her eyes were tight in anger. Fists clenched, she felt nothing but contempt for the weak-chinned innocence of the man.

Bring to boil and simmer for 45 minutes to one hour.

She had barely seen him after that – an odd glimpse on the streets of Maransay or, perhaps, a snippet of news in the pages of the *Chronicle*. Their reports would tell of him giving talks and short sermons, preparing for the day he would enter the ministry. She remembered once seeing his photo in its columns, standing with two other men who had gathered clothing and food to give to some orphans in Eastern Europe. She looked up to see Allan, his own son, standing at the bars of his playpen, a rattle tight within his hand.

Once she had spoken about him. A neighbour, Jessie Macleay, had heard him speak in a local church. He had given his testimony – an account of his life till God entered his existence and how it changed thereafter.

"What did he say?" Cathy asked, her voice trying to conceal her concern.

Jessie took a long time before answering, her fingers dabbing the traces of Coffee Cake staining the edges of her mouth. "Oh, the usual... How he used to drink a lot. Even use drugs sometimes. How he used to carry on with married women."

"Did he mention which ones?" The words almost stumbled to Cathy's lips, but she stifled them in time. Her eyes focused instead on young Allan playing with Moira in the garden; the two children looking so unalike that people searched for ways to explain their differences. *"Oh, he's so much like*

you... And the others. They're the spit of Colin. " It was for their sake that her silence would continue. There would be no dramatic moment when – as he preached his first sermon in his Church in Marnwick at the south end of the island – she would charge down the aisle, dragging Allan behind her as she yelled out her accusations. Instead, she would remain in her home, making sure it was a good one for her family, cleaning, cooking and preparing meals like the platefuls of soup which she would:

Season and serve with bread or rolls.

And she would be content with that existence. Or at least she would certainly try to be.

The Restoration

"Memory is the only paradise to which we can escape."
From a leaflet introducing the work of the Irish artist,
Michael Sheehy, at the Crawford Gallery, Cork, Summer 1995.

"Why don't you paint?" His friend Bill's words on the phone were all he remembered of Sunday. "You used to tell me you did that when you were younger. Wouldn't it help you pass the time now?"

James peered into the mirror in his bedroom as if his own gaze might give him some answers to these questions. A lined and puckered face stared back; bloodshot eyes within its folds. Hell! He looked bad. And of course all around him, there was the staleness of drink and cigarettes; the stench of clothes worn far too long; untidiness and dirt; his own sense of decay and hopelessness filling every corner of his home. The expression on a neighbour's face had made him aware of all this when she had come to the house the other day.

"Is there something off in here?" she had asked.

Cheeky bitch. But the question touched some part of him still untainted by all the rot and self-pity he had suffered since Cathy had died. Angrily, he tossed his empty bottle of whisky into the bin. She had always said he would come to this – if she wasn't around to take care of him.

By the following Tuesday, he had bought brushes, paint and canvas, setting up his easel in the kitchen his wife had wanted for their years of retirement. And he started to draw what he saw outside his window. The darkness of the winter sky shadowing the harbour with its breakwater half-demolished by the force of the Atlantic. The low black cliffs with their rocks engulfed by the whiteness of waves. The windswept sheep on their bare pasture. The gulls reeling. And in the foreground, a modern kit-built house built for a family of incomers on the site of an old black house. Its front wall was a mosaic of differing shades of bricks; its driveway grey, its ornate gate brightly painted.

Home after years of working in the Clydeside shipyards, sights like these had troubled him. They did not belong to his village – not to a place that had stayed unchanged in his memory. Even on canvas, their presence seemed an intrusion, as if their light and modernity were at odds with the old and muted shades of their surroundings. He paused as he stood there, and began to score it out – with whisky glass in one hand and brush in the other, blacking out its walls – until the entire scene became an angry blur of loops and straight lines.

Like a black hook, memory dug into him as he sat drinking that night. He remembered Hector, the old man who had stayed in that black house, seeing him with his father one day they had come together to thatch the roof. They were dressed in denim jackets and dungarees – his father looking much the same age as he did now, but wizened and tough where he was larger, softer, even paler. Clutching hay-forks in their hands, they piled billows of straw high upon the roof, pressing and combing them flat with their prongs.

"It'll be your job to restore this one day," his father said, speaking in that low, snide voice James had always thought belittling. "We won't be around to do it." He turned to place another load way up on the ridge, narrowly missing his son's face with the points of the prongs.

And then that vision changed. It wasn't hay with which they were covering the roof, but fire. Yellow flames first of all, followed by plumes of red, as if there were a blaze raging around them. He tried to tell them to stop, running back and fore at the foot of its walls, his arms flailing, but the older men didn't listen, piling on one burning layer after another. A short time later and he couldn't see them any more, his vision obscured by the smoke of their labours.

He woke up sweating at his fireside, another empty half-bottle at his feet. His mouth dry, he padded to the kitchen, passing the canvas on his way. He noticed the scrawl he had done the night before, deciding then how he might complete it. He would draw Hector's old house where the new one stood, the greyness of its walls and thatch blending with the landscape in a way its modern replacement would take an eternity to do.

Over the following days, the village of his past took shape once again below his brush. The broken breakwater that sheltered the harbour was healed, stretching out into the ocean as it had done years before. A few boats lay upturned nearby, tied for the winter with their hulls black and secure with tar. The fields were filled with grazing cattle or sheep with a blur of red or blue on their backs. There was the green, too, of oats and turnips and potato fields.

"I'm painting the whole place from my memory," he told his mate, Bill, on the phone the following week. "Restoring it to what it used to be. The good old days, eh?"

But somehow, after he had finished, the picture lacked conviction. He stared at it for a long time before deciding why. There were no people anywhere. The road, the fields, the harbour – each one was empty of men or women. Finally, he drew a tiny female figure in the doorway of Hector's house. He grinned, recognising the old man's wife, Marissa. She was in one of her usual positions too, standing at the doorway or the window with her blue eyes squinting behind her glasses, eagerly noting everything that might be going on.

He had hated her when he was younger. "Old Buzzard-Bitch" he called her – especially for the eyes that never seemed to miss anything that was going on. And there was also the way she seemed to swoop directly to a parent's door with tales of the mischief this or that child had done.

"Do you know what he's been up to?" she would screech.

His father always reacted angrily when she came to their home. His hands would reach for the belt he always tugged around the waistline of his dungarees.

"Is this true what I've been hearing?"

But he put this out of his mind as he sketched the figure, drawing the brown scarf she wore around her head, her slippers and apron. She was larger now than she had ever been in reality, the dominating mistress of her home.

After this, James spent as much time on the figures as the scene. There were the old men standing at the whitewashed wall of the Post Office: Alasdair Gow with his sleeves rolled up, his sailor's tattoo on his right forearm; Ruaraidh with his wife's shopping bag at his feet, the butter he had purchased having melted by the time he reached home; the tall, olive-skinned figure of Sandy bending to spit a mouthful of black tobacco from the pipe he clutched in his hand. And as he drew, he could hear their conversations – the words of men who had died years before, during the time James had spent in Glasgow.

"When I was in Africa..." Alasdair would begin.

"I suppose it's time I went home now," Ruaraidh might say, reluctantly prising himself away from the conversation.

And Sandy's talk was always coarse and lewd. He'd see a woman coming up the village road to the Post Office and instantly, these grey eyes of his – protruding a little with their eyelids not quite fully open – would be alive and active. "How would you fancy a go on that one?" he'd say. "No' bad, eh?"

It was this last man – an old bachelor – who had shown him his first picture of a naked woman. His large hand, soiled by nicotine and work, had taken a set of sepia-shaded photographs out of the top pocket of his denim jacket, couching one in the light. James' eyes took in the strangeness of the female body; her long dark hair, sweep of breast and thigh, nipples like strange and remote stars, the secret shadow between her legs.

"What do you think of that then? Does it do anything for you?"

Sandy's face was close to his own as he asked the question, the old man's breath warm on his cheek and the weight of his fingers on his shoulder.

James' own hand trembled at the memory, paint smearing the canvas as he smudged the line he had been working on. It was because of this he decided to set his painting aside for a time. Leaving the house, he struggled head down against the strength of an early Spring wind, regretting he had been misled by the warmth of his home and not put on enough layers for comfort. In the old days, there had been no such problem. People woke in the dark in cold rooms, shivering as their toes stuck to the lino. Downstairs, dampers were shut, ashes scraped; each sound a jarring reminder of the wind and weather.

He turned into the Post Office – a small building that also served as the village shop. A family of Glaswegians who had moved recently to the area were in there, squabbling over what sweets the children might be allowed to buy. Almost in reaction, he found himself ordering a bottle of whisky.

"Needing some inspiration?" Seonaid the postmistress said.

He laughed weakly in response. Looking around the village, there was almost too much. The old water-mill down at the river where people used to gather now stood motionless and still. The walls of Murdag's house – which she had tried to keep as it had been in her father's day – had crumbled with its roof, doors and windows gone. Farquhar's home was now used as a barn, rust-brown chickens entering and leaving one of its doorways. The buildings which had once been full of people now just had ghosts which only he could see.

When he got home, he began to draw the bus that had driven through the village when he was young. It was a black, single-deck Morris with a wooden frame; Angie Thomais was at its wheel as it stood at the road end, waiting for the passengers to enter. Mairi Mairead was in the doorway, wearing her usual black widow's dress as she creaked her way up the steps. Ronnie stood behind her, and then following him there was his older brother, Neil. His hand tugged the heavy brown suitcase that contained all his belongings the day he left home.

He had never seen his brother since that time. The next he heard, Neil was working in a car factory in Coventry building, perhaps, one of the buses in which he left home that day. After that, he was dead – killed as he stepped out from behind one into the path of an approaching car. The body never came home; the family hearing of a wife and child they had never dreamed existed before. It was their wish for Neil to be buried somewhere near them – in a cemetery in the Midlands – not these islands off the north-west coast of Scotland.

Slowly he began to draw in the details of his brother's face: the tanned, curved forehead; curly brown hair; deep-set light-coloured eyes; a full mouth rather sulky and proud. As he did so, he began to recall there were other aspects to his features that day. His mouth had been cut, dried blood at its edge. His cheek was grazed.

And his eyes held the defiance of a young man who had decided to set his boyhood aside.

"Don't let that drunken bastard put his hand on you," he had told James.

But the drunken bastard had. He remembered only too well how it happened. A few days after Neil had left, he was trudging the village road. Sandy came towards him, his pipe in his mouth. When he smiled, his teeth were almost as brown as his fingers.

"No doubt you're missing your brother," he said. "Well, we all will. He's a fine, young lad. This place has lost too many like that."

"Thanks," James nodded, displaying his emotions as clearly as any teenager might – his face grim and heavy, his mouth set in a frown.

"I'll tell you what…" Sandy's fingers unbuttoned the top pocket of his denim jacket, taking out his set of pictures in his hand. "That should cheer you up. Put the pep back in your pecker for a while."

He laughed as he brandished them, his grimy thumb on the face of a headless body whose breasts and thighs, clad only in long black stockings, hypnotised James. His heart raced as he took this all in, gazing round, too, to make certain no-one was looking, that the likes of Marissa wasn't squinting in his direction from the window of her home. And then his hand rushed out to accept Sandy's offer, shoving the photographs into the pocket of his jacket.

"I'll expect them back at the end of the week," Sandy grinned. "Unstained and in virgin condition."

And the older man's laughter echoed as he walked away, his footsteps quick and lively on the village road.

James took them out that evening in the quiet of his bedroom, spreading them out in a fan-shape on the blankets of his bed. He took in every detail of their appearance: the dark lipstick some wore; the hair crimped or long and flowing, brunette or blonde; breasts large or small; the Japanese woman; the coloured girl; the Swedish...

He began to draw one, taking out a picture from the pack. It was of a young brunette kneeling on crumpled sheets. Her hands were on her thighs; an inch or so above the only item of clothing she wore, a tiny garter. Her black hair was uncombed, mouth slightly open. Her breasts jutted outward. As his pencil moved across the paper, seeking to imitate the curves and flow of her body, he failed to hear his father enter the room.

"What the hell are you up to there?"

His father had a drink taken – the stench of his breath told him that – and it was always when he had a drop, he was at his most righteous and sanctimonious, his hand lashing out in a vengeful fury. James knew this from long experience, and he scurried the pictures under his blankets, desperate to hide them from the judgment of the older man's gaze. But he failed to do this. Within seconds, a few were in his father's clutches.

"Who gave you those?"

James didn't need to speak. The answer to that question was already in his father's mouth.

"Sandy! Don't you have enough sense to keep away from that man?"

It was then the inevitable happened – his father tugging open the belt around his waist.

Years later he still remembered the terror of that beating. The buckle of the belt scraping against his skin. Blood. Bruises. Pain. The feeling that everything worked against him. Always had and always would. Nothing could change that. Not his painting. Not his years away. Not his wife, Cathy. Not his return home. Not even another bottle. Much though he pretended that might help, that might straighten him out.

Despite the memory, he began to paint, replacing the canvas he had on before. This time, it was another drawing done from his recollections. A sketch of his own young face distorted and twisted by pain. In it, he portrayed his own tears and anguish, the torment he had suffered when young.